"[This] compelling tale carefully leads us to a conclusion that is both rewarding and—unusual for Sallis' tales about Griffin—uplifting."
—*Los Angeles Times*

"[*Eye of the Cricket*] is an anthology of great scenes, great images, and great dialogue."
—*Kirkus Reviews*

"The novel's cadences are reminiscent of the poetry that Sallis also writes, and it reverberates with past tragedies and hope for the future. It is the fourth volume of a collective masterpiece."
—*The Pilot* (North Carolina)

"James Sallis is a fine writer with sheer artistry in his painting of word pictures."
—*The News-Sentinel* (Knoxville)

"No private eye can compete in the philosophy department with Lew Griffin, the creation of poet, essayist and novelist James Sallis. . . . This is not so much a mystery as it is a meditation on the mystery that is life."
—*San Jose Mercury News*

"Sallis' tale is mesmerizing. . . . To say that [his] effort is simply noir is an understatement."
—*State Journal* (Lansing, Michigan)

EYE OF THE CRICKET

EYE OF THE CRICKET

A Lew Griffin novel

JAMES SALLIS

WALKER & COMPANY

NEW YORK

First published in the United States of America in 1997 by
Walker Publishing Company, Inc.

Published simultaneously in Canada by Fitzhenry and Whiteside,
Markham, Ontario L3R 4T8

Library of Congress Cataloging-in-Publication Data
Sallis, James, 1944–
Eye of the cricket: a Lew Griffin novel/James Sallis.
p.   cm.
ISBN 0-8027-3313-1 (hardcover)
1. Griffin, Lew (Fictitious character)—Fiction. I. Title.
PS3569.A462E9   1997
813′ .54—dc21   97-24375
CIP
ISBN 0-8027-7581-0 (paperback)

Printed in Canada
2 4 6 8 10 9 7 5 3 1

To Karyn
again, and always.

Then I felt within me the desperate
rebelliousness of things that did not
want to die, the thirst of mosses, the
anxiety in the eyes of the cricket. . . .
                    —Enrique Anderson Imbert

EYE OF THE CRICKET

1

THE STORM CAME in over the lake, bowing the shaggy heads of young trees and snapping branches off the old, blowing out of Metairie where the white folks live. In my own backyard a hundred-year-old water oak at last gave in, splitting in half as though a broadsword had struck it, opening like a book.

I sat with my back bent over the worn mahogany curb of the bar. A glass of bourbon sat before me, its outer surface smeared and greasy to the touch. A young roach circled water pooling about the glass.

Astonishingly, what had begun as a letter to an old friend, to Vicky in Paris, had become the opening pages of a novel. The first real writing I'd done in over four years, though a novel not so much new as reimagined. And so I had moved from lined legal pad and kitchen table to a long-neglected computer out here in the slave quarters behind the house.

I paused a moment, sipped at bourbon. It was midnight, it was raining. I glanced out the window and went on.

For a long time we were quiet. The man beside me raised his glass and drank. Traffic sounds fell from the freeway arching above us like a cement rainbow half a block away.

"Life is cruel, old friend, *n'est-ce pas?*"

His shoulders rose and fell in that peculiar shrug only the French, even Louisiana's long-relocated French, seem able to bring off.

Boudleaux had come to tell me that my son was dead, needlessly, stupidly dead. Though in fact there had been no need to tell me. I had known from the way he entered, his pause in the doorway, light splaying its broad fingers on the bar, what message he brought. Probably I had known all along.

Again he shrugged. In the bar's mirror, our two hands raised glasses, held them momentarily aloft. We watched as they moved towards one another. No sound: had they really touched?

We drank.

It wasn't bourbon in my glass, but nonalcoholic beer, Sharp's. Four years since I'd done much real writing. Four years since I'd had a drink. Somewhere along the way, a lot earlier than I wanted to think about, alcohol's smile had become a grin, then just bared teeth. Whole chunks of my life had fallen into that maw. Friends, intentions, memories, years.

"And nothing to help us but a few hard drinks and morning."

"*Rien.*"

He raised his hand for the barkeep.

Wind tore the door open then. Trailed by teenagers, a brass band playing "Some of These Days" passed in the street outside. The door swung shut. I heard the grill's hiss from back in the kitchen, the click of billiard balls, automobile horns far away, a sports report from the radio beneath the bar. Upstairs, where there were apartments, a toilet flushed, and flushed again before its tank had a chance to refill. That sudden light had blinded us all. Now gradually the room, this stray, gray corner of the world, came back to us.

The phone rang.

I read the last line or two, keyed in ALT-F and S, and leaned over to turn down the volume on Son House's "Death Letter Blues." She a good ol' gal, gonna lay there till Judgment Day. The computer chirred briefly to itself. Outside the window, a spindly orange spider coursed along a web that was visible one moment, invisible the next, as the spider's motion carried it into and out of moonlight.

"I'm sorry to bother you at this hour." A voice that sounded like a lot of my students. Young, not from New Orleans or the South, reluctant to release (in a way you sensed more than heard) the ends of words. "We're trying to reach a Mr. Lewis Griffin. The author?"

"This is Lew. What can I do for you?"

"Excuse me, sir. You're the one who wrote *The Old Man*?"

"I'm afraid so." But it had gone permanently out of print, like many of our civil liberties, sometime during the Reagan-Bush dynasties.

"All right!" He turned to speak to someone, turned back. "This is kind of complicated."

I waited.

"Mr. Griffin, my name is Craig Parker. I'm a fourth-year medical student currently assigned to the emergency room at University Hospital."

"That's Hotel Dieu, right?"

"Used to be. Yes, sir. I guess people around here, lots of them, still call it that. What I wanted to tell you— Excuse me." After a moment he came back. "Listen, this may be really off the wall, but we have a guy down here in Trauma One, a garbage truck backed over him. Driver says none of them ever even saw him. Hard to tell how much damage the truck did, anyway. He'd already been beat up pretty bad. Left there in the alley, the police figure."

"This is someone I know? He told you to call me?"

"No, sir, he's not able to tell us anything. We're doing what we can. But it's not looking good."

"Then I don't think I understand."

"Yes, sir. Well, as I said, it's complicated. And a real long shot. Excuse me a moment, sir." Someone close by him spoke insistently. He responded, listened, responded again. Then he was back. "Sorry. Things are pretty hectic down here. All we need now's— Shit! Mr. Griffin, can I call you right back? Two minutes, tops."

"Sure."

It was closer to twenty. I sat watching the cursor blink on the screen before me, checked out the spider's catch, listened to Blind Willie, Robert and Lonnie Johnson—blues night on WWOZ. I thought about Buster Robinson, dead, what, ten, twelve years now? Singing the refrain of "Going Back to Florida" in a club on Dryades when a bullet meant for someone else dissected his aorta and left him suspended forever on the seventh. I'd learned a lot from Buster. A lot about the blues. Later on, more important things.

"I do apologize," the young man, Parker, said when he rang back. "Here's what I called about. The guy I told you got run over, *worked* over before that, he's a John Doe. Brought in with no name or ID. Nothing. But afterwards one of the nurses thought to look through his clothes piled in the

corner and found a paperback book in his back pocket. Looks like it's
seen hard times same as he has. That, or he's had it awhile."

"The Old Man."

"Yes, sir. There's an inscription on the title page. 'To David.' Then
something in Latin—"

Non enim possunt militares pueri dauco exducier. The sons of military men can't be raised on carrots.

"—and your signature."

Two hands, one of terror, another of hope, tore at my heart.

"Can you tell me what your patient looks like?"

"Afro-American male, probably late twenties. Six feet or so, I'd say,
maybe just over, and lean. Athletic build. Brown eyes, hair cut short.
Maybe with a knife, from the look of it. Clothes ill-fitting, much-used,
but cleaned not too far in the past. From one of the churches or missions,
maybe."

I reached out to shut the computer off. This was one thing I could
do. One thing in the world that I had control over. The computer asked
was I certain this was what I wanted to do. I hit N.

"Would it be possible for you to come down here and have a look,
Mr. Griffin? Tell us if you know him?"

"All right," I said, with little idea which I wanted, to know him, not
to know him. I again hit ALT-F and X. Then Y for changes, and Y again
to confirm my intention to leave Windowland.

The computer beeped once, twice, blinked out at me, shut its systems down.

Growing quiet at the same moment WWOZ and its announcer fell
silent between songs.

"Just come to the triage desk out front, right inside the doors, and
ask for me, Craig. Any idea when you might be getting here?"

"Depends on the cab situation. Within the hour, anyway."

"Great. We really appreciate this, Mr. Griffin. See you shortly,
then."

Music gave way to public-service announcements. A music-and-
books raffle at the local Unitarian-Universalist church. A Celtic Weekend
two weeks hence. Free AIDS testing.

I finished my glass of Sharp's, looking out at the nebula of spiderweb
floating aslant in the darkness, then at the photo on the wall across from
the desk.

It was the only thing in the room hinting towards any effort at decoration. Richard Garces had given it to me: a snapshot he'd taken of LaVerne when they worked together at Foucher Women's Shelter, a month or so before she died. She'd stuck her head in the door to ask a question about one of his clients and been trapped there forever. Smiling and at the same time instinctively trying to turn her head away. A Verne I'd not known at all, really. Richard's lover Eugene, successful fashion photographer by trade, starving fine-art photographer by inclination, had cropped and enlarged the snapshot.

For ten years, so long and often that I no longer really think about it, I've told this story to my students, Michelangelo's definition of sculpture: You just take a block of marble and cut away whatever's not part of the statue.

That's what our lives do. Wear away what's not part of the sculpture. Pare us down, if we're lucky, to some kind of essential self.

Or to some hardened, unconsidering icon if we're not.

LaVerne and I had met when we were both little more than children and had gone on chipping away, sometimes together, sometimes apart, most of our lives. No one had been more important to me; my life was inexorably linked with hers. And yet there was no one to whom I had been less kind, no one, among the many I had hurt, whom I had hurt more.

Once Verne said to me, "We're just alike that way, Lew. Neither of us is ever going to have anyone permanent, anyone who'll go the long haul, who cares that much." But she was wrong. In the last years of her life, years during which for the most part I never saw her, she got off the streets. She educated herself, became a counselor and the quietest sort of hero, helping retrieve others' lives even as she ransomed her own. She fell deeply in love, married, and was on her way to reuniting with lost daughter Alouette when a stroke struck the last blow at the marble. By way of saying farewell and the many thank-yous I'd never had time for, I searched out and found Alouette, but after a time she, like so many others, had gone away.

Gone away as had David, my own son. Into the darkness that surrounds us all.

It occurred to me now that LaVerne may well have been the finest person I've known.

Individually, collectively, we struggle to rise out of the slough of ourselves, strive upwards (like a man trapped in water beneath ice, swimming up to the air pocket just under, where at least he can breathe) towards something better, something more, than we truly are. That's the measure of grace given us. But few of us individually, and seldom does the collective, manage it.

Leaving, I turned off lights, threw the switch that shut down power to the slave quarters. Stopped off in the kitchen to open a can of tuna with egg bits for Bat and have a glass of water from the tap, then walked three doors down, to where, as usual, the bright green DeVille taxi sat out front.

"Father home?" I asked the young man who came to the door. Rap's heavy chopped beat and nervous legato lyrics filled the room behind him. He wore jeans so oversize that they hung on his hips like a skirt, crotch down about his knees, bottoms lopped off. Sixteen, seventeen. Head shaved halfway up, hair like a woolly shoot above. All ups and downs.

"Yeah," he said.

"Think I might speak to him, Raymond? That possible?"

"Don't see why not."

Norm Marcus appeared behind him, peering out. He wore baggy nylon pants, a loose zipped sweatshirt, shower cap.

"Lewis. Been a while. *Thought* I heard the door."

"Raymond and I were just saying hello."

"I bet you was. Well, Cal and me, *we're* just sitting down to break-fast." I never had been able to figure when this family slept, what kind of rhythm they were on. "Why don't you come on in and join us? There's plenty of food, and we can always find an extra chair somewheres."

Then to his son: "You want to step away now, Raymond, give us some room here?"

The boy shrugged and returned to the couch that, near as I could tell, he lived on. He was surrounded there by stacks of CDs, half-eaten packages of chips, Pepsi cans, pillows and a blanket.

"Thanks, Norm. Some other time. Soon. I promise."

"You need a ride."

"Afraid so. But look, you're about to eat—"

"No problem, Lewis. Just wish we'd see you sometime when you could stay a few minutes. Where we going? So I can tell Cal how long I'm gonna be."

He stepped into the kitchen and was back at once.

"Let's roll."

From his couch Raymond carefully ignored our departure.

"I apologize for taking you away from your family and your dinner, Norm," I said as we turned onto St. Charles, "but it's important."

"You wouldn't of asked, otherwise."

He took Jackson to Simón Bolívar, turned onto Poydras. The hospital was surrounded by stretches of vacant lots behind chain-link fencing. As he cut between two of them, I said, "I think my son's in the ER."

He nodded. "Hurt bad?"

I told him I didn't know. Neither of us said anything else until we pulled in at the hospital.

"You want me to come inside with you, man? Or wait out here?"

I shook my head. "But thanks."

"Anything I can do, you let me know."

"I will."

"Tough, huh?"

I'd started away when he called out: "Lewis." He leaned down into the passenger window so we could see one another. Put a closed hand to his ear. Call me.

One might have expected to see Craig Parker, with his elegantly understated clothes, blond hair and strong features, in the pages of a fashion catalog rather more than in this chaotic, bloody, antiquated ER. Yet, surrounded by junkies and drunks, gunshot wounds, knifings, crushed limbs and cardiacs, the breathless, he seemed strangely at home here—calm and in control. A rare fortunate man who had found his place in the world and begun to flourish.

He thanked me for coming, turned to a woman nearby and said, "Cover for me, Dee?" Three other people were all talking to her at the same time. "Sure, no problem," she told him.

"Come with me, please, Mr. Griffin."

We went down a hallway straight and narrow as a cannon.

"Something I need to tell you. Bear right, here, sir. . . . Shortly after we spoke, the patient arrested. He came back pretty quickly, but whenever the bottom drops out like that, it's a tremendous shock to the system. We've put him on a respirator, chiefly to take some of the strain off his heart. It—"

"I know, Dr. Parker. I've been through this before." Searching for

LaVerne's daughter Alouette, first I had found her premature baby, on a ventilator in a neonatal intensive care unit up in Mississippi. Alouette herself had been on one for a while.

He nodded. "I wanted you to be prepared. Most people aren't. Here's the book, before I forget." He pulled it from one bulging side pocket of his lab coat.

The cover was all but torn away, mended top and bottom with Scotch tape. A horseshoe-shaped section like a bite was gone from the lower right corner. Cover, spine, pages, all were filthy, mottled with a decade and a half of spills.

I hadn't seen a copy in years but, holding it now, I remembered —with a physical lurch of memory and an instinctive motion to save myself, as though about to fall from a precipice—the day I sat writing the final chapter.

I pushed the door open and saw his back bent over the worn mahogany curb of the bar. I sat beside him, ordered a bourbon, and told him what I had to.

For a long time then we were quiet.

"He's in here, Mr. Griffin."

Through the open door I saw several people standing over a gurney. On it lay a nude, catheterized young man. One of the workers was between us, and I couldn't see the young man's face. A bright green ventilator stood by the wall, squeezing air into him through plastic tubes that danced with each respiration. Other, smaller tubes snaked down from poles hung with bags of saline and medication. Tracings of his heartbeat, respiratory pattern and blood pressure stuttered across the screen of a monitor overhead.

"Anyone called for a pulmonary consult?" one of those in the room asked.

"They're all up on pedi, one of the hearts went bad on them. We're next on the list."

I looked around, back along the corridor. There were windows far away, at its end. Lots of windows. Rain washed down them all.

2

THAT WAS TUESDAY. The day before, our tenth straight day of rain, I made it to Modern European Novel almost on time and, standing in the doorway soaked and adrip, was surprised to find the room filled with students.

Water boiled up everywhere out of the canals and drainage system, streetcars and buses ran irregularly if at all past businesses closed down from flooding, large animals, small cars and children were being swept away, and still these kids showed up to talk about literature.

My childhood bends beside me, too far for me to lay a hand there once or lightly: Stephen Daedalus at his teaching. But these (as I kept reminding myself) weren't kids, and comparing our childhoods didn't even make it to apples and oranges.

I remember a musician friend, a guitarist, telling me he got gigs mostly just because he made them, because he always showed up. That was pretty much how I'd wound up teaching English Lit. Who's taking Modern European Novel this semester, with Adams off in Berlin? the chair asks at a department curriculum meeting. And someone says how about Griffin over in Romance Languages, *he*'s a novelist. Does a great job with Modern French Novel. Next thing I know, I find myself on temporary trade, like a ballplayer.

How much of our life occurs simply because we don't step backwards fast enough?

So I find myself quoting, instead of Queneau or Cendrars or Gide, feeling an impostor the whole time, Conrad, Beckett or Joyce. Surely they'll find me out.

I added my own to the line of half-furled umbrellas aslant against the back wall. Like firearms on a stockade wall, strange trees growing upside down out of pools of water.

"Last class, we were talking about Ellman's biography of Joyce." I pulled out my folder of notes. Water dripped along my sleeve into the satchel's interior. Three spots fell onto the folder itself, raising small blisters.

"In another context, and of another writer, Ellman remarks: 'If we must suffer, it is better to create the world in which we suffer. And this, he says, this is what heroes do spontaneously, artists do consciously, and all men do in their degree.'

"Never has there been, I think, a more determined world-creator than Joyce."

Today we were discussing the Nighttown sequence from *Ulysses*. In past weeks I had sketched out for them the basic structure of the novel and stood by (I hoped) as they discovered that not only was the book fun to read, it was actually funny: No one ever told us *that* before, Mr. Griffin. Probably not. *Ulysses* was offered up to them, to us all, as some kind of intimidating monolith, like those giant gates in *King Kong*. You had to beat on the drums and chant the right formulas before you'd dare let the beast of Literature loose.

Hosie Straughter had told me about the book years ago. When Hosie died of cancer in '89, body withering down in a matter of months to a dry brown twig, I couldn't think of a more appropriate tribute than to sit that whole weekend rereading *Ulysses*. Literature was only one of the things Hosie had given me. I had my own beasts. Hosie showed me how to contain them.

"The sequence is phantasmagoric, equal parts dream or nightmare and drunken carousing, Freud, E. T. A. Hoffman and vaudeville all whipped up together in the blender. Here, more than anything else, it resembles Beckett's work. Like Beckett's, it's about nothing—and at the same time about everything.

"All the novel's characters and relationships, all the novel's *figures*, one might even say the whole of civilization—"

"Prefiguring *Finnegans Wake*." Mrs. Mara. In the front row and a denim miniskirt today.

"Exactly. In the Nighttown sequence all these characters and relationships—real, mythic, imaginary—reappear, maybe *resurface* is the best way to put it, in various transfigurations."

"Even historical figures like Edward the Seventh," Kyle Skillman said. Limp blond hair, face forever red as though recently scrubbed. A yoke of dandruff when he wore dark clothes.

"Or Reuben J Antichrist the wandering jew." What was this one's name? Taylor, Tyler, something like that. Couldn't remember his ever speaking up in class before.

"But why?" Skillman finished. His aching for a world where everything *fit* could break your heart. I found myself wondering, not for the first time, if he might be in some kind of emotional trouble.

"Anyone want to answer Mr. Skillman's question?" I looked around the room. Eyes sank to the floor as though on counterweights. "Mrs. Mara?"

"Obviously dreams are a kind of art, our most personal expression. One of the ways we make sense of our world."

"Or, in a sense at least, re-create it: yes."

Mrs. Mara swung her leg at all of us in approval.

I, for one, beamed at our collective brilliance. But Skillman still looked worried. Loose pieces everywhere.

"Let's look, then, at this most telling of resurfacings from the Nighttown sequence: the sudden appearance of Bloom's dead son, which ends it.

" 'Against the dark wall a figure appears slowly, a fairy boy of eleven, a changeling, kidnapped, dressed in an Eton suit with glass shoes and a little bronze helmet, holding a book in his hand. He reads from right to left inaudibly, smiling, kissing the page.' "

And so our discussion continued for most of the hour, rain slamming down outside, pools of water from umbrellas flowing into one another, Sally Mara helping urge reluctant students from point to point like some fine intellectual sheepdog.

Near the end, Kyle Skillman put down a well-mashed, half-eaten tuna sandwich to raise his hand.

"Sir, you haven't told us when the first test will be."

"I wouldn't worry about that just now, Mr. Skillman. There will be a final, at least; perhaps a midterm. Let's just wait and see how things shape up. I'm sure you'll all do fine, whatever.

"Next week, we'll look briefly at Joyce's *Wake*—no, you're not expected to read it—and segue towards Beckett's *Molloy*—which you are.

"If there are no further questions, I'll see you all on Wednesday."

I replaced my notes in the satchel. Their own went into briefcases, book bags, folders and accordion files, backpacks.

One by one, umbrellas left their posts at the back wall.

"Mr. Griffin?" someone said as I stepped into the hall. "You have a minute?"

Older than most of them, hair cut close, black suit giving him a vaguely Muslim look. Collarless white shirt buttoned to his neck. Left hand curved around a history text. He held out the right one.

"Sam Delany."

"You're not one of my students."

"No, sir. Though I would be, if my schedule weren't so tight."

"Walk with me? I'm heading for my office. Russian history, huh?"

"I needed another history elective. It fit between Theories of Modern Economy and Dynamics of the Body Social IV. I'm pre-law."

We went down the stairs and into a storage room the school insisted upon calling my office. I shared it with another part-timer who fortunately never used it. You got both of us lodged in there, and a student by the door, I don't know how any of us would ever have gotten out.

"So what can I do for you, Mr. Delany?" I waved him into the chair across from the desk. He was thin enough that he almost fit there. Idly clicked on the computer to see if it might be working today. Nope.

"I've heard a lot about you, Mr. Griffin. You're kind of a hero to some of the students, you know. They look up to you."

I had no idea what to say to that, so I kept quiet.

"I was born across from the Desire projects. First sixteen years of my life, I looked out the window, that's all I saw. Never guessed the world could be any different. Hard to relate to professors with their tenure and Volvos and their nice, safe homes out in Metairie. But you're not like them. You're still *out* there. Always have been."

"Not for a long time."

He shook his head. "I read your books. Some of them are hard to find."

"Some of them probably ought to be a lot harder."

"They tell the truth, Mr. Griffin. That's important."

"Yeah. . . . I used to think so too."

"That they tell the truth, or that it's important?"

"Both." I looked out my so-called (*soi-disant*) window, a sliver of glass set sideways just inches below the seven-foot ceiling. Rain had slowed to a drizzle; there was even a hint of sunlight. "You want to get some coffee?"

"I'm from New Orleans, Mr. Griffin. I'm *always* ready for coffee."

"Able to find a chink in your tight schedule, then?"

"Well, I tell you. Right now you *are* my schedule."

We crossed from the campus to a corner grocer that had four-seater picnic benches set up in the back half of the store and from ten till they ran out served some of the best roast beef po-boys, jambalaya and gumbo in town. Most of the kids stuck to burgers and fries. A student once told me that she'd lived off burgers since she was fourteen, never ate anything else.

As always, Marcel's was a thicket of noise: formulaic greetings (*How it is, 'S up, All right!*) as people came and went, the singsong of conversations at tables, orders taken on the bounce and passed off to the cooks in verbal shorthand, music from portable radios the size of cigarette packs or toolboxes, the occasional shrill, monotonous Morse of a beeper.

We got coffee in thick-walled mugs and snagged a table just as two business types, coatless but wearing short-sleeve blue dress shirts and ties, were getting up. Delany wiped off the table with a napkin, piled everything on the tray they'd left behind and took it to a hand-through window near the back. Both the window's broad lip and a steel cart alongside were ajumble with bowls, trays and cups.

"So just what is it I can do for you?" I said as Delany sat across from me. Over his shoulder I read the wall-mounted menu, one of those black boxes with white plastic letters you snap in, like setting type. Halfway down, they'd run out of O's and substituted zeros. Sandwiches were offered on *Bun or French bred*. Elsewhere there were curious gaps and run-ons.

"You find people."

Sometimes, yes. But as I'd told him earlier, not for a long time now. I'd let teaching become my life, drifted into it because the currents were flowing that way. I wondered again how much of our life we really choose, how much is just following chance road signs.

"I take care of my family," Delany said. "Financially, I mean. My father disappeared when I was four. The other kids' fathers—I have one half brother, fifteen, two sisters, eleven and eight—they disappeared a lot faster. I look out for them all."

A familiar story, though never one the conservative axis with its one-size-fits-all "family values" wanted to hear. The poor, the fucked up, disadvantaged and discarded, are an awful lot of trouble. If only they'd *behave*.

"And your mother?"

"She's still with us. Alive, I mean. It's been hard for her, she's . . ."

"Used up."

"Yeah. I guess that says it, all right."

"She the one you wanted to see me about?"

He shook his head. Looked over to the line by the counter. "More coffee?"

I pushed the cup towards him and he brought it back full, with just the right amount of milk. He'd watched me closely earlier, but I hadn't thought much of it at the time. This peculiar intensity hovered about him anyway, as though details were a lair where the world lived, coiled like a dragon; as though everything might depend on our noticing, on our taking note.

"My brother," he said. "Half brother, really. Shon: like John with a *sh*. Older girl's Tamysha, with a Y. One of the nurses named her that when she was born. Little one's Critty—god knows where *that* came from. Anyway."

He took a mouthful of coffee, held it a moment, swallowed.

"One day last week, Thursday, Shon leaves for school same as every morning, scooting out of the house half-dressed and already half an hour late. After school he's scheduled for the four-to-eight, so no one's looking for him till late—"

"Where does he work?"

"Donut shop up by the hospital."

"Touro?"

"Yeah. And sometimes one of his friends would drop by the store about the time he got off and they'd hang out awhile, so it might be ten, eleven before he showed up home. But that night, ten comes and goes. Mama's home by then—I stay with the girls while she's at work—but we still just figure Shon'll be along any minute. Next morning, couldn't of been later than six, not even light outside yet, Mama's at my door with the girls."

"Shon was a no-show."

"Right. Mama fixes us all breakfast, and when Shon's school opens up at eight—I tried to call earlier, and got no answer—I go down there. Not only wasn't Shon in class the day before, I find out, but he hadn't been there for two, three months. And you didn't notify anyone? I say. We just figured he dropped out, the teacher told me. He's *fifteen*, I tell her. Yeah I know, she says, lots of 'em don't last *near* that long."

"That was it?"

He nodded. "Not a ripple since."

"Have you talked to his friends?"

"I tried. Turns out the ones I knew, kids I remembered being his friends, he hadn't had much to do with them, or they with him, for a long time. He must have others, but I haven't found them."

"Not a good sign. People change habits and friends like that, usually it means a lot more's changing."

"Yes, sir. I know."

"I'll need the name of his school, kids you already talked to, his teachers, anybody you know who works with him, usual hangouts, particular interests."

He took a manila envelope out of the book and passed it across to me. The photo inside showed a light-skinned, smallish, compactly built young man with prominent features and hair clipped almost to his scalp. He could easily be in his twenties. The rest was details. Names, lists. Nouns with no verbs. Like the photograph: bits of information, points of light, outlining a presence, a shape, no longer there.

Sudden as pain, memory struck: a twilight long ago. I was twenty, new to New Orleans. Carl Joseph had gone off one of the roofs he'd used to shoot people from, and his mother had come to me to try to make some kind of sense of it all. Having told me about her son, about his life, she walked up the path around the big house into darkness, and I thought: Another person leaving, falling away.

Then another memory, another blow. Years later. I'd just told the Claytons their daughter was dead and watched them turn to stone. A friend of Verne's named Sanders had killed himself, filming the whole thing. Verne and I were sitting together on her couch, looking out the window and drinking.

I used to ride trains a lot, Verne said. Mama'd put us on one and give the conductor fifty cents to look after us. And I'd sit in the end car and watch everything pass by, all those places and people I'd never get to know, gone for good—and so quickly.

I'm still on that train, Verne told me. I've always been. Watching people I've loved go away from me, for good.

I slid everything back into the envelope. Phone numbers were on the outside. His own rented room, his mother's apartment, the university library where he worked most evenings.

"I'll do what I can," I said.

"I appreciate this, Mr. Griffin."

"Don't expect too much. And what there is, is likely to be bad."

That afternoon I visited his half brother's school, his mother at work, and the donut shop at Prytania and Louisiana.

One of the shop's glass doors had been covered with plywood, permanently from the look of it, and wired shut. A cardboard placard on the wall warned, NO Alcoholic Beverages on Premises. Notices on the remaining door and on the marquee beneath the TAST-T DONUT sign outside read Open 24 Hrs. Come in here at two A.M., you'd find people in layers of old clothes sitting half the night over a cup of coffee.

The kid behind the counter with a shock of hair like carrot tops shooting off his head and wearing a dough-smeared assistant manager tag confirmed that Shon Delany had failed to show up for work last Thursday. He'd also missed his shift on Friday, and again on Sunday. Nor had he called in, any of those times.

Shon's homeroom teacher, a Miss Kamil Brown, couldn't be more specific about when Shon had stopped attending school. I'm sorry, she kept saying. Sorry she couldn't help me, sorry she hadn't tried to contact Shon's parents, sorry she didn't have any real reason to call attendance, sorry she didn't have time to get to know the students any better. I believed her sorrow. She was in her early twenties, couldn't have been at this more than a few years. Already she looked about her as though unable to remember how she got here, or exactly where *here* was. Her eyes and voice were affectless, like those of young soldiers.

At RiteWay Dry Cleaners on Baronne the boy's mother, Rachel Lee Baldwin, reiterated what Sam Delany had told me, admitted that Shon hadn't been talking to her much these days when she *did* see him, and said that she had to get back to work. She too, whether from this latest incident or her whole life, had a vague, shell-shocked look about her.

That night after dinner at Dunbar's I walked down Carondelet into town and prowled the Quarter awhile before settling in at the Napoleon House. Joe's closed down years ago, the Seven Seas is long gone, but the Napoleon House is still around, looking pretty much the same as it always has. Still has the same pictures, and as far as I can tell the same coat of paint, it had when I first saw it.

I sat there watching those around me, those walking by past the French doors that opened one wall of the bar to the sidewalk outside, and thinking about a passage from *Ulysses*.

The sadness, the dark, in Dublin late at night, Joyce wrote, is swingeing. People who do not want to go home, who will not go home, who have not got a home, lurch and stagger in the gloom, moths without a candle.

About nine an off-duty cop who turned out to be a friend of Walsh's came in. We got to talking about the murder rate and the new mayor, wondering if the city would ever haul itself back upright.

Hours later, though I'd had only coffee and club soda, I lurched and staggered home myself.

3

I REMEMBER A December, unseasonably warm—it might have been June. Sometime in the late sixties. Cataclysms everywhere: social, racial, personal. The whole period's kind of a blur. Not a good time for me, as they say.

I'd been thrown out of yet another apartment, spent the night in a covered bus stop having intermittent, elliptical conversations, and at eight, when it opened, was standing outside the K&B at St. Charles and Napoleon waiting to buy a pint of bourbon. Someone else was there before me, a neatly dressed businessman type in his Lincoln with the windows up and radio on. He asked for two pint bottles of vodka, and at the register, for just a moment, our eyes met in silent kinship: two men buying liquor at eight in the morning.

I walked along St. Charles sipping from the bottle, watching cars surge forward a half-block, a block, before they fetched up at a dead stop behind traffic. Hydrogen sulfide burned on the air like a fuse. I turned off to the right, lakeside, into stands of massive old houses painted white, light blue and peach. Palms, hibiscus, yucca trees and rubber plants sat in terra-cotta pots on galleries, balconies, patios. Rooms behind windows were sparsely furnished with antique sofas, paintings in ornate frames, chairs and tables adrift on rafts of tapestrylike carpet, chandeliers clear and bright as springwater. An area where a black man had best keep moving.

By ten-thirty or so, bottle long depleted, I was heading back downtown towards Louisiana. A young man stood outside Gladstone's hosing off the parking lot and street. In better days I'd stop at the lounge there for a drink whenever I was in the neighborhood. Louis Armstrong used to meet fans and friends at the Gladstone when he came back to town.

Getting close to noon. Lunchtime. Between St. Charles and Claiborne I walked by at least a dozen corner grocery stores, bars and one-room cafés, all of them giving off the meaty, rich smell of frying shrimp that's so much a part of this city. I had no place to go, and I was hungry. But what I wanted most of all was another drink.

There was a period back then when I lived for over a year on something like $400. Rent for a small apartment, a kitchenette and one room, maybe even a tiny bedroom, was $75. I'd pay a month's rent and move in. Wouldn't be able to make the second month, but they wouldn't throw me out till the third—then I'd move on. At first, each new place was a step down the social scale. Later on they seemed more like steps down the evolutionary scale.

I'll never forget the last one. I rang the front bell, and up from the stairwell of the basement where she lived rose a storklike woman, flanked by three dogs, whose skin had peeled away in patches, leaving narrow dark septums around white flesh.

The apartment's floor was warped. Linoleum in spots had fused with the floor's wood; missing boards held in place windows (themselves missing panes) beyond which hung screens orange with rust, screens so brittle that pieces broke away when I touched them. The hot-water heater squatted in a corner behind the couch. Pipes in the wall drummed furiously whenever anyone flushed a toilet or ran water. But it was all I could afford, so I took it. I paid, moved in my two paper bags stuffed with clothes and books, drank a celebratory six-pack and fell asleep. About three that morning I awoke to a languid, warm breeze through which stars shone brightly and a light rain fell, and went out.

And that was it, I never went back there. The next time I awoke it was in a hospital with this guy's face six inches from my own saying, "Hey, bud, you in there?"

Don thought I never knew how bad it got, but I did. Drinkers always know. We've just turned ourselves into experts at not noticing. All those years, almost every night, I'd wake at two or three in the morning, heart pounding, to the call of sirens across the city. A mass of vines swinging in the wind would make a hunchback, human-shaped shadow on the wall, or rain in the trees would sound like the feet of a thousand small living things coming towards me in the dark outside. Naked and sick, I would stand at the window, promising myself the whole thing wasn't going to start up again, thinking *I won't*, knowing I would.

One of those nights, one of those mornings, at a bar on Magazine—it's been a long siege—a guy next to me is talking. For how long, I can't remember. Can't remember much at this point, just these few moments. But he seems to be in the middle of something.

So I just moved up the street, he says, took that whole crowd with me, mothers, sons and all. I tell you, those were the days. Never *will* be another time like it. That old horn's bell crinkled up something fierce from all them times I'd bang it 'gainst the floor to get those boys' attention, but then whenever I'd lift it up, point those few first notes at the sky, it was like all of a sudden the whole *city* was holding its breath, listening. And pretty soon they'd start coming down from uptown, and from over by the river, from *all* over. Didn't need to put up signs. Those first notes were all it took.

To this day I don't know how much of the encounter I imagined. I had had, by that time, more than a few conversations with people who weren't there. Maybe it was only some local musician telling me about his life and, playing novelist even then, picking at the pieces of his story, arranging and rearranging them, I came up with this guy claiming to be Buddy Bolden. Maybe it was all just a hallucination. Or one of the dreams that ripped me from sleep at three in the morning.

I remember how light gleamed and swam in the bottles behind the bar as I turned to him. I've always wondered, I told him. When they carried you off to the madhouse. People said it was because you threw a baby out of an upstairs window.

You know well as I do, young man, people be likely to say anything. 'Sides, it was one of them skinny close-built houses down on Jackson. Woman in the next house, she saw what was happening and jus' put her arms out and *caught* that baby.

You miss it? I said.

The music?

I nodded.

Everything done changed now, son. Tell you the truth, most days I miss the barbering more.

Then he was gone.

I walked down Claiborne, past the smell of yet more frying shrimp, to Loyola and then to the library, where I spent the afternoon reading Borges and watching people board and dismount buses outside.

Fleeing reality?

You better believe it. Feeling its hot breath on my neck.

I remember how intense, how alive, things became as the sun sank low. Tables, chairs, corners of shelves, roofs across the street—all trembled, faintly luminous, as though fragments of sunlight, reluctant to let go, still clung to them. Lambent.

But it was not only the visual world that came so strangely into focus. Moments before the library closed, I heard a reference librarian's voice as she spoke into her phone half a building away: "Here's the information you requested, sir. He died in Concord, at 7:05 A.M., May 21st, 1952. That's right, 7:05. You're welcome."

Out, then, into the waiting, impatient street.

4

"I'LL HAVE THE red beans and rice," Richard Garces said. "Please tell me they're not left over from Monday." Monday was traditionally washday in old New Orleans, fix-ahead pots of red beans and rice simmering on the stove. Many restaurants carry on the tradition. It's a city that embraces tradition.

"Tuesday, at the latest," Tammy said. One high, jean-clad hip went higher as she rested hand and order pad on it. "No reason you'd notice, but we do move a little slow around here."

They barely moved at all. Moochie's reminded me of those time capsules they used to bury back in the fifties, full of artifacts: a newspaper, recordings of popular songs, comic books, Kool-Aid packets, a nylon scarf, souvenir ashtrays. Neon clocks and beer signs hung on the walls. Formica, fake-wood paneling and bright plastic everywhere. Hank Williams, Patsy Cline and Jimmy Reed on the jukebox.

We did our best, Richard, Don Walsh and myself, to get together like this at least once a week. Have dinner, talk things over. Sometimes it would get put off week after week, other times it might happen every day or two. Over five or six years, I guess, it averaged out.

"And to drink?" Tammy said.

"Coffee."

Don ordered rigatoni, salad with Italian. "And a beer. Any kind." I looked at him. He shrugged.

I asked guiltily for a large Caesar. Blood work on my two most recent hospitalizations, over a year ago, had shown high cholesterol, but I tried not to think about it.

Iced tea now, coffee after.

"Tammy. How's Byron?" Richard said.

She had started away towards the kitchen, a turn, two steps; and now turned back. Hip again rising as she shifted weight onto one leg. A kind of all-purpose gesture for her, at the same time confiding and defensive.

"He's fine. Said to tell you hello in his last letter, now that I think about it."

"Still in Atlanta?"

"Oh yeah. Couldn't haul him out of there with a team of Clydesdales."

At college in the sixties, both of them impossibly young, Richard (as they used to say) had brought Byron out—or they'd brought one another out. Then they'd openly lived together for a number of years. Something people throw parties and send out invitations for, nowadays. But back then that sort of thing was your own personal Pearl Harbor. It was underground nuclear testing in your backyard, Commie infiltration at the DAR, dry rot in the moral fabric.

"Still with Chip?"

"You bet. They finally bit the bullet. Got married last year."

"And your folks?"

She shrugged.

"Maybe with time," Richard said.

Tammy's glance said no way, there *wasn't* that much time. She dropped our order off at the kitchen.

"So it wasn't David after all," Garces said, returning to the conversation Tammy had interrupted when she came to our table.

"No. Though it could have been."

"Assuming David is still alive," Walsh said.

I nodded. Of course. "But in some very odd, very particular way, it *felt* as though it were David—when I first got the call." I tried to explain what was going on within me as I walked into that room. Warm fronts and cold fronts colliding, high-pressure areas, patches of dazzling sunlight, scatters of raindrops the size of cities.

Tammy brought our drinks.

"No way to explain the connection?" Richard said. "What he was doing with David's book?"

"No way to know there *was* a connection. He'd had the book a long time. Someone had."

"I take it there wasn't any ID on him."

"I sent a lab tech out for prints," Walsh said. "Lots of mental hospitals routinely fingerprint their admissions. He's been on the streets long—and it looks like he has—then chances are good he's in the system somewhere, a match is going to roll up."

"I was at the hospital all night. About noon, he stabilized and got shipped upstairs to one of the ICUs." It had looked like some futuristic version of *The African Queen*: three people pushing along his raft of a gurney hung with clear plastic bags, monitors, oxygen tank, respirator the size of a lunchbox. "He's since regained consciousness. But he was anoxic during the arrest. No way to know how long, really. Or how much damage was done."

"This may be just another dead end, Lew."

"Maybe."

David had disappeared years ago, during a summer in Europe. In effect he fell off the edge of the world. He'd written his mother almost every week, then the letters stopped. Two months passed. Her own letters to him, sent *poste restante* to a post office in Paris, were never returned. I tried to trace him: got Vicky and her husband in Paris to run things down at that end, talked to the chairman of his department and to David's sole friend at Columbia, had an old friend of my own, a detective in New York, follow up there. Dooley was able to place David on a nonstop flight, Paris to New York, then to a cab that dropped him midtown, maybe Grand Central or Port Authority. There the trail went cold. Dead ends.

It was *all* dead ends. I had put the minicassette with its two twenty-second segments of blank tape where someone had called, stayed on the line, and said nothing—whenever I heard them, trapdoors fell open beneath me—away in my desk.

"They're pulling the tube tonight," I said as Tammy brought our food. "If he's able to remember, able to talk at all, I'll find out what the connection is with David."

"Assuming there is one."

"Right."

"Get you anything else?" Tammy asked. We told her no. She told us to enjoy.

"You want me to come along, Lew?" Walsh said.

"No need. I've spoken with the doctors. They say it's okay."

"I'll be home. They give you any problem, you call me." He downed the last half of his Abita Amber in a single gulp and started in on his food. Forkful of salad, forkful of rigatoni.

The smell of Richard's red beans came across the table in waves. A plateau of rice jutted above the beans at one side of the bowl, a section of sausage, striped black from the grill, at the other.

"Something else." I told them about Shon Delany and asked if either had any suggestions.

Walsh shook his head. "Lew, you ever gonna learn to say no?"

"No."

"I'll get it on the network tonight, if you'll write it all down for me."

I already had, and handed it across. Richard was part of an underground information system, social and mental-health workers who'd more or less stumbled onto this as an effective shortcut. He'd used it before to help me find LaVerne's daughter.

"And tomorrow morning I'll talk to some of the people on the streets, slide them into it. Kids especially."

"Thanks, Richard."

"*Es nada*. Speaking of which," he said, turning to Don, "the streets and kids, not nada: how's Danny doing?"

Walsh shrugged.

"No job yet?"

"Jobs were rain, he'd be cactus. He did work half a day at a place on the butt end of Canal, one of those old diners that looks like a trailer. The manager, kid about ten years younger than him, started to show him how he was doing something wrong and Danny just walked out. Showed up at the house still in his apron."

"I figured things weren't going too well when he missed our lunch last week."

"Days go by when I hardly see him at all. Others, a block and tackle couldn't get him out of the house. What can you do?"

"Not much, Don. Tough as it is."

"Yeah."

One night last year Walsh had got a call from the Coral Gables, Florida, police department. An officer there said they had his son in custody. The charge *this* time (yes, they'd had him at the station before)

was burglary. Twenty-eight years old, Danny was still living with his
mother, unemployed, the officer said, and recently, while she was away at
work and he off somewhere, his mother's house had been cleaned out. An
investigating officer tracking stolen goods came across her TV in a pawn-
shop and, following up on it, days later trailed Danny back to the self-storage
facility where he'd cached his mother's property. He'd pawned a few things,
given some of it away, but mostly it was just sitting there, stacked up neat
as a pin.

The boy's mother now claimed that she might have kind of given
him permission, or at least somehow given him the impression that it
would be perfectly okay, to haul off the furniture, appliances and even
the handles off the kitchen cabinets for chrissake. So, unless she decided to proceed, beyond a court-ordered commitment for observation,
there wasn't a lot they were going to be able to do—till the next time.
But his, Walsh's, name had come up during the investigation, and now
Sergeant Montez was calling as a professional courtesy, officer to officer,
because he thought Walsh might want to know what was going on, maybe
get involved?

The upshot being that when Danny got out from under the commitment, he decided he'd be better off living with his father. Well, not
actually living with him, he'd just be in the same city, you know. So he
came to stay with Don while he looked for work and a place of his own
and never left.

Big brother-like, Richard had taken him under wing, showing him
the city (not that he seemed much interested), introducing him to a few
people (in whom he seemed even less interested), meeting him for occasional lunches and coffee.

"Tell him to give me a call," Richard said.

"I will."

"Anyone up for dessert?" Tammy asked. "Sam's put together a sweet
potato and pecan pie that he plans on advertising as a threat to intelligent
life on the planet."

Most cities, they leave it up to traffic, poverty, automatic-weapons
fire. Things like that. Here, they try to feed you to death.

We declined.

"Coffee all around, then?"

"With a shot of bourbon and another of these." Don held up the
empty Abita bottle. When Tammy brought everything on a tray, he drank

his coffee at once, then threw back the bourbon and started in on the beer, nursing it. It was a door I'd spent a lot of years ducking to get through, myself.

"So you're headed back to the hospital," Richard said.

I nodded.

"How about you, Don? You got anything on for tonight?"

"Go home, see if Danny's there, see what shape the place's in. The usual."

"I'm hitting the seven o'clock show at the Prytania, you want to come along."

"You asking me for a date?"

"You bet, big boy."

"Probably some damn French thing, too. Get me in the mood."

"Oh, I thertainly hope tho."

"You guys want anything else? Nah, thanks, Richard. But I think I'll go on home. Not much in the mood for lighthearted comedies."

"Actually, according to reviews it's a gripping, compelling tale of obsession and madness."

"Well then. I definitely don't need any more of that. I get gripped and compelled real hard, every day I go in to work. Most nights too, I don't turn the phone and the beeper off."

Tammy put the check down. I reached, but Don already had it.

"My turn."

Outside, everything about the night was quietly transformed. Humidity softened the edge of buildings; glistening wet, the streets looked clean and new; even the headlights of oncoming cars were wrapped in shells of soft white. We walked together a block or two, to Don's car, the same ancient Regal he'd had for years. Richard continued up Prytania.

"Drop you, Lew?"

"Thanks, but I'll walk. Great night."

He looked around. "Yeah. Yeah, I guess it is. Let me know how things turn out at the hospital?"

"Don." He'd gotten in. I leaned down to be at a level. "You going to be all right?"

"Sure. Sure I will. We always are, aren't we, you and me?"

"It's been a long siege, my friend."

"Yeah, just sometimes I get tired of looking at the goddamn white of their eyes, know what I mean?"

I nodded and shut the door for him. He looked through the window at me a moment, then rolled it down and stuck out his hand. I took it and we shook. It seemed an odd thing to do with so old and close a friend.

I watched him drive off, into the night. Thinking I'd walk partway then get a cab, I cut over to St. Charles and wound up, instead, walking the whole distance.

The upper parts of buildings were gone, as though, from the sky down, everything were slowly dissolving, slowly becoming insubstantial. Cars materialized beside me all at once out of the mist. Buses loomed up like sudden cliffs. Walking across Jackson to Claiborne, I came upon two men sitting together in the shelter of a cardboard box shouting a tuneless duet. Even their words, as far as I could tell, were invented.

After all, Beckett says, when you're in the last bloody ditch there's nothing left but to sing.

5

HIS EYES WENT from the doctor's face to mine, back and forth. They were wholly without emotion or recognition, without *presence*, lifeless and flat as lentils; and otherwise he made no visible effort to move. His arms lay out beside him on the bed. His feet had thick, horny undersides, as though sandal soles had been grafted on. The toes turned in.

He was probably older than he looked.

"You can talk now, sir. Though you're going to have an awfully sore throat for a while. Can you tell me who you are?"

The doctor's name was Bailey. He bent to hang an oxygen cannula over the man's ears and adjust it. Straightening, he looked across the bed at me and shook his head.

Through two narrow windows set together in a corner I could see only the mist roiling outside—not even the city's lights. We were on the third floor.

"Can you tell me what day it is, sir? Do you know where you are?"

Just those eyes, arcing back and forth.

That blankness.

"You're going to be all right. You've had an accident. You're in the intensive care unit at University Hospital. You came in last night, Tuesday. So this is Wednesday." He paused. "*Now* can you tell me where you are?"

He waited a moment. Still nothing.

He turned away.

"I don't know. Looks like we're definitely going to need a neuro consult."

He dropped the endotracheal tube with its cluster of tape into a wastebasket beside the bed, went to the sink and squirted Betadine from a dispenser mounted on the wall. Started washing his hands.

"You want to page the medicine intern for me? I'm getting no breath sounds on the right," a nurse called from one of the beds across the room. At the central desk a unit secretary picked up the phone. "Also a stat chest and an ABG."

Bailey stepped from behind the partitioning curtain. "I'm already on the unit," Bailey said. "Excuse me, Mr. Griffin."

He went across to the bed and, after listening a moment with his stethoscope, asked for something. The nurse passed him a syringe. He tapped at the man's ribs a time or two, then, holding the syringe like a dart, jabbed it into his chest.

"Pressure's going down. O$_2$ up to 84."

A second nurse came over carrying a bundle, pushing a bedside table. She set the bundle down, tore open the tape sealing it and unfolded greenish-gray material from around a stainless steel tray, coils of rubber tubing, surgical instruments in clear sterile packages.

With one of those instruments Bailey punctured the chest again just below the syringe. With another that looked like a combination between cooking forceps and needle-nose pliers he threaded a rubber tube into the chest, stitched it in place, and attached a plastic bottle.

A chest tube, for pneumothorax. At one point before she died, Baby Girl McTell, Alouette's baby, LaVerne's daughter's baby, had five of them.

"Okay, looks good. Let's get a stat chest to confirm. Good catch, Nancy. ABG when you're ready?"

The nurse was listening to the man's chest. She glanced up and nodded, moved her stethoscope to the other side. The second nurse was tossing instruments into the tray, disposables into the trash.

Bailey came back across the floor.

I nodded towards the man on the bed between us. He hadn't taken his eyes off Bailey the whole time. Now the eyes swung to me. Still, empty, depthless. Like shallow water. His face, though deeply lined, with hard planes and full features, somehow just as emotionless, just as blank.

The word *wiped* came to me. Then a flurry of synonyms: erased, undone, deleted, obliterated, expunged, dissolved, consumed.

Bailey again shook his head.

"Always hard to say, especially at first, with cases like this. The trauma itself can temporarily short-circuit everyday connections. And sometimes people come up with really weird responses to emergency drugs. He was beaten on the head. Almost certainly there's been some degree of anoxia. We don't even have any way of knowing what kind of shape he was in *before* all this."

Again he began scrubbing his hands at the sink.

"We'll watch him. I'll have neuro in for a look. Not much else I can tell you right now. Could be a whole different ball game by morning."

He'd hung his lab coat on the end of the bed. As he reached for it, the man on the bed said, "You got my book."

We both turned.

"What?" Bailey said.

"My book. You got it."

"He was carrying a book when he came in," I said. "They found it in his clothes downstairs."

"Who are you, sir? What's your name?"

"You got my book."

"We have to know who you are, sir."

"You got my book," he said. Then, politely, added, "Sir."

I got the book from the inside pocket of my coat and handed it to him. He took it: the first time he'd moved. He looked at the front cover, turned it over, opened it and looked inside. Then he looked at me and nodded.

"My book."

And that was it. He closed his eyes and fell asleep.

I moved out to the waiting room where, mostly alone, I passed the night watching the dreary banter of talk-show hosts and guest celebrities, a rerun of *The A-Team* in which the boys defended a Vietnamese grocer in East L.A. from marauding Latino gangbangers, a couple of movies whose plots, characters and climactic car chases were indistinguishable.

There might be no connection at all between David and this patient, of course. He could simply have found the book somewhere; come across it in curbside trash, a basement, some abandoned room or building.

I wasn't sure I wanted to think too closely about where or how he might have found it. For a long time now, years, when I thought of my son at all, I had assumed he was dead.

But this man might have found the book at a shelter of some kind, maybe in New York; it could have made its way there, even been left there by David himself. Or at a church, the kind in which people take refuge, the kind that hands out blankets and feeds the destitute, keeps a cache of Bibles and books and old clothes on hand for them.

Last night in ER—no, it was night before last now—Craig Parker had suggested that the patient's clothes, apparent castoffs but recently cleaned, might have come from one of the churches or missions.

Around twelve the guy polishing the floor shut off his machine, got a thermos of coffee from his cart, and started telling me about the house he and his girlfriend were buying up on Valence. Needed some work, sure, but he could do that himself, take his time and do it right, meant they were getting a real bargain. Been looking a long time. Not many bargains left anymore. He just loved those old shotguns. Only problem was it was next door to a cemetery, and he wanted to know if that would bother me. I told him I loved cemeteries.

Twenty-year-old sitcoms for an hour or so then. Fred Sanford had the big one. J. J. strutted around his family's project apartment explaining his latest scam.

Starting about two-thirty, a security guard walked by three times within the hour, finally stopping to ask could he help me and who I was with.

Not much choice after that. (1) Religious programming. (2) News repeating itself over and over like a stutter. (3) The last half of a movie from 1938. Pick one.

Around five a nurse on break sat beside me and, smoking three cigarettes in fifteen minutes, told me the story of her life. Sadly it wasn't much of a story *or* a life, and she knew it.

As I watched dawn take over the window, it came to me that I had utterly missed my Wednesday classes—not only missed them but not even given them a thought. It was the first time in years anything like that had happened. Since I'd gone looking for Alouette.

At seven a bleary-eyed, much-bespattered Bailey got off the elevator. He came up to me and stood staring out at the light.

"Been here all night?"

"Yeah."

"Hope *you* got some sleep, at least."

I shook my head.

"Must be something in the air. Well, let's go see what the morning's brought, shall we?"

I followed him into the unit. Nurses were changing shift, walking from bed to bed as they gave report. The ones going off looked used up. The ones coming on didn't look a hell of a lot better. Sunlight streamed in at the windows, glared on every surface. Workers pushed carts of linens and supplies through double doors. The phone buzzed and went on buzzing.

Behind the half-curtain he sat almost upright in bed. A plastic wash-basin and soap dish were on the tray table before him. He was nude. A towel covered his lap.

"Cleanliness. Next to," he said. "Any moment now. I'm marshaling strength."

His eyes went from Bailey to me and back. He smiled, and one hand lifted in a sketchy, exhausted wave.

"Good morning. Early start on the day, huh? I didn't expect you this soon."

He looked closely at Bailey.

"You wanted to know my name."

Bailey nodded.

"Lewis Griffin," he said.

He held up his ragged copy of *The Old Man*.

"My book. One of them, anyway."

6

SO THERE I was in an old yellow T-shirt and the white boxers with hearts on them that Richard Garces gave me as a joke. Squinting out at these huddled shapes. Streetlight on the corner working for the first time in months.

"Norm?" Some others, too. My God, it must be serious. Raymond's forsaken his couch to come along.

"Lewis. Apologize for disturbing you this time of night. Woke you up, too, from the look of it. You know Janet Prue? Lives two houses up, on my side."

I didn't, but nodded. Late sixties, early seventies. That classic tweed-and-khaki look. Silky gray hair.

"Janet: Lewis. And this is Janet's husband, Gene. Lew Griffin."

All shapes accounted for.

"You think we might come in for a minute, Lew? Won't keep you long."

I stepped back out of the doorway. Your perfect host. Meanwhile something German and very loud was playing on the radio I'd neglected to turn off when I went to bed. I turned down the volume.

"Please have a seat."

Still knew how to act when company came, after all this time.

Mr. and Mrs. Prue sat on the couch, Norm and his son in chairs close by.

"I guess I'm here as a kind of representative." Norm glanced at the Prues. "Speaking for a lot of your, our, neighbors.

"You may not know what's been going on, Lewis. Have to be busy with your teaching, and writing all those books—can't imagine how much time *that* takes. And I know you like to keep to yourself, of course, value your privacy. We respect that. It's part of what makes the neighborhood work. *Any* community.

"So we apologize again for intruding on you."

He looked over at his son.

"And for waking you up," Raymond said.

"Can I get you folks anything?"

Four heads went no. Good. I didn't have anything to get them.

"Last few weeks there's been a team of robbers, purse snatchers, working the neighborhood. Kids really. Riding bikes and carrying guns. They held up one of the college girls down the street last week. Big house where all the students live? She waits tables in the Quarter two or three nights a week, took the streetcar home to Napoleon and was walking the rest of the way. Had the night's tips on her, just under a hundred dollars. Now, she thinks she remembers seeing them circle by once or twice before they pulled up at the curb, but at the time she didn't think anything of it. Who would? Then they pulled up by her, flashed the gun and told her to hand over her purse.

"There've been at least a couple more. Last night Janet and Gene were late for—some kind of alumni dinner, right?"

They nodded.

"Janet came out, got to the car and realized Gene wasn't behind her anymore, and went back in to check on him. He says he'll be right there, so she comes back out and stands by the car. Porch light's on. She doesn't remember seeing any bicycles going by, no. But all of a sudden, there they are. One of them's got a passenger on the back. He leans over—like Indians going from side to side on their ponies in old movies, she says afterwards—and snags her purse. Strap pulls tight and snaps, she reaches, but it's gone.

"I *could* use a glass of water, it's not too much trouble."

I brought him one from the kitchen. Even found a clean glass.

"We're talking black here, Lewis. You understand that? Black kids on bikes with guns, hitting their own neighborhood. Ours. Never mind the robberies, that's bad enough. But sooner or later someone they pull up beside's going to talk back, or else someone looking out his window is going to go get *his* gun, next thing you know we've got a street full of police cars."

"Okay, Norm, what do you want me to do?"

"I don't know. But everybody on the street knows you're a detective—"

"Used to be."

"Used to be, right. So anyway, they thought maybe you'd have some idea how we could get on top of this. Thought maybe you could check around, ask some questions."

"What kind of questions?"

"You'd know that better than us. Meanwhile, we're handing this out to everyone in a six-block radius."

He passed me a sheet of standard typing paper, computer generated.

```
         IMPORTANT MEMO! DISTRIBUTE IMMEDIATELY!
There has been a rash of armed robberies in this part
of Uptown New Orleans in the last several weeks. At
least 4-5 have happened in our area alone.
The perpetrators are Negro male juveniles, 12-16 years
old in school type uniforms—white shirts and khaki pants.*
They go about in groups of 2-4 and are armed with at
least one blue steel revolver. The time frame of the rob-
beries is after school until 8 P.M. They ''case'' the area
first—walking or riding bikes up and down the block—
then approach the intended victim with a question, i.e.,
What time is it? Victims have been walking home or
sitting on their front porches.
WE MUST BE VIGILANT! Do not allow these juveniles
to engage you in conversation—this is a DELAY TACTIC
to SET YOU UP AS THEIR NEXT VICTIM!
Be even more careful getting in and out of cars
and entering your home.
If you see a suspicious group of juveniles as described
above, call 911 immediately.

* NOTE: Pants may be gray in color.
```

"We've already handed out over a hundred of them," Norm said.

"Okay."

We do like to feel we're useful. Still, I couldn't help but think of all the grocery-store ads rolled into cones and tucked into my fence out front, restaurant to-go menus and housepainting specials rubber-banded to my door handle, real estate fliers stuffed illegally in my mailbox. Guys got half a cent apiece to distribute these and lived off the three or four dollars a day the work netted them. A fictive economy held aloft by its own bootstraps, one that few people noticed or gave thought to.

"I'll keep an eye out, Norm. That's really all anyone can do—even the police."

"Good enough." He stood. So did the others.

"Thank you, Mr. Griffin," Mr. Prue said.

"We appreciate this," his wife confirmed.

Pillar of my community, for sure.

Norm's son lingered behind.

"Something I can do for you, Raymond?"

"Nah." He stood watching my rear wall. Anything happened back there, it wouldn't get past him. "My civics teacher says it was someone named Lew Griffin who stopped the guy that shot all those people from buildings back in the sixties."

"Mmm-hmm."

"Says he hunted the guy down and threw him off the top of one of the buildings."

"I think I heard about that."

"Yeah. Lots going on back then." Raymond looked at me. His father called from outside. "Don't guess that was you, huh."

"Must have been another Lew Griffin."

"Yeah. Yeah, that's what *I* said."

I shut the door behind him and turned up the music again. Bach, a prelude and fugue, Wanda Landowska at her monster harpsichord, plucking the world back into order.

Visitors gone, Bat shot down the stairs and sat mewing, waiting impatiently for me to provide an appropriate lap. No question which Lew Griffin *he* wanted.

The one that was here.

7

WHAT I WAS doing was counting, reduced by circumstance (liberals would say) from loftier aspirations—social conscience, the humanities, the pursuit of literature—to simple mathematics.

There were 3 of them. I'd been hit 9 times, kicked 4. I had 1 loose tooth. It was 1 o'clock. This was, would have been, my 3rd stop.

I was also remembering: my mind in defense breaking free, floating above it all, recalling all those *other* times. Thinking that this sort of thing never happened to Proust, never sullied *his* remembrances. Give me a madeleine any day.

Maybe the things that happen to us are things we make happen, things we somehow attract.

Maybe all failures are failures of will.

Maybe I ought to stop getting my butt kicked.

Not that I held it against them personally. Fifty-year-old guy wearing a tie and coat, guy no one ever saw before, looks like a cop but he's not or he'd be flashing ID, shows up in the neighborhood asking questions. What else he gonna be but bad news, a repo man, skip chaser, collector of some kind? Sure as hell ain't from the IRS. And looks like he might have a few dollars on him, weighing him down? Civic-minded young brothers just naturally gonna help the man out, provide him some answers. Natural as rain.

But enough's enough.

It was a trick, a technique, I hadn't had occasion to use in years.

Like all technique, at first it happened instinctively. Only later did I ask myself just what was occurring and how. Then I broke it down, from initial impulse or stimulus to response and final result, prodding at disjointed segments, plotting the curve. Building a grammar. It had to be reproducible.

You reach down and find the rage, the frustration, defeat and despair, find that black pool just beneath the world's surface that never goes away. You find it, you bring it up, you use it. For a while it takes you over. You become its vehicle. What voodoo practitioners call a horse.

I turned onto my back, grunted with pain, gasped and held my breath. They all pulled back a moment, and when the one at my feet leaned in for a closer look, I kicked him between the legs. Then spun on my back and took another's legs out from under him as he was looking up to see what happened to his man. That left one standing—but only till I'd slammed my foot straight into the side of his knee. The others would get up, in time. He wouldn't. The second guy was already trying to get up. I gave the side of his head a light kick.

Afterwards, this strange serenity comes over you. The vessel's emptied, no more fright-or-flight, but adrenaline's still got your senses racked up high. Everything's incredibly sharp, clear, intense. The world shimmers. You hear breathing from an upstairs apartment, a birdsong blocks away. You see patterns of sunlight in the air around you. You hear a cat moving, crouched down low, against the wall. Sirens screaming miles away in the CBD. Boat horns on the river.

That's how it was as I walked back up through the Marigny and Quarter towards Canal, senses ratcheting down like a car on a jack. In others' faces I saw the ordinary world returning. On a clock's face I saw it was almost two.

Morning had been narrative oatmeal: all expository lumps. I'd got home from the hospital planning on a few hours' sleep before I dropped by the school to patch things up and took another shot at tracking down Shon Delany. Never in my life had I wanted a drink more. I settled for coffee. No way caffeine was going to keep me awake. I'd have slept through the Inquisition.

But I only slept through thirty minutes. Fumbling for the phone. Seeing my coffee cup, still full, on the floor by the bed.

I'd been promising myself for some time that I was going to go buy furniture, a bureau or two maybe, bookshelves, some kind of table for beside the bed. A lifetime spent tucking belongings underarm and moving on leaves odd habits. I'd lived here now for over ten years. Chances were fair I'd stay awhile.

"Lew?"

I realized I hadn't said anything. I'd just picked up the phone and lay there with it to my ear, listening.

"Mmmmhn."

Much better. Civility rears its shaggy head.

"Want me to call back?"

"You at work?"

"Yeah. City's funny that way, likes me to show up on a more or less regular basis."

"Give me five minutes."

"They're yours."

I drank the cold, grayish coffee, splashed water on my face and stood at the window for a couple of minutes watching the world hunch its shoulders towards another day. Since it was Thursday, garbage was set out near the street for collection. A woman in a motorized wheelchair rolled from can to can, combing through each, pulling out select items that she dropped in a canvas bag strapped to the back of the chair.

Don, wonder of wonders, was actually at his desk and answered when I called back.

"Must be a slow day."

"Aren't they all. I just said the hell with it, I'm taking a break. Sit here and watch the goddamn storm go on happening."

"They still trying to kill everybody in the city?"

New Orleans had clocked 421 murders for the year thus far. Even the folk out in Jefferson Parish were getting concerned, as violence spilled towards their precious suburbs. I kept expecting them to announce any day that they were putting up a wall.

Don grunted. "This rate, it'll take them what, ten, twelve years till no one's left? Hang on, Lew." He spoke brusquely to someone, then was back. "Wanted to let you know nothing's come in on the prints or photo. Not that I expected anything, this soon." His voice rose suddenly. "You want to wait a fucking minute? What, you think this is my lunch, I'm eating the fucking phone? No. *I'll* find *you*.

"You still there, Lew?"

"Yes*sir*."

"Cute. Okay, I talked to the officer who took the call, but he couldn't tell me much of anything we don't already have. Call came in, nine-one-one, at nine-fourteen, from the driver of the sanitation truck. No real evidence of struggle—"

"How could you tell, *our* alleys."

"Right. Obvious that the truck hadn't been the first thing after him that night, though. No evidence that he, or anyone else, was living in the alley. Could have just wandered in there, or been dropped there afterwards. No sign of personal property or belongings, aside from what he had on him. I've got a copy of the report here for you, you want it."

"Thanks, Don."

"No problem. How'd it go at the hospital?"

Long and shallow. The man stuck resolutely to his story. He was Lewis Griffin, a novelist who wrote about what it was like on the streets, about the city's real, subterranean life. Self-taught. A primitive. Working on a new one now. He'd done three chapters just that morning.

You mean yesterday morning, I said.

Whatever. He'd fixed himself a light lunch, some leftover roast pork with creole mustard on pumpernickel. Had a couple of pickles and a Corona with it. Then he'd gone out for his usual afternoon walk and somebody must have jumped him, because that was all he remembered.

I asked him where he lived.

Uptown.

Been there long?

Ten, twelve years. He told me about LaVerne, how they'd once lived there together, but that was a long time ago. Some days everything seems a long time ago, he said.

I asked him to tell me about his books.

You haven't read them, then?

I'm afraid not.

He shook his head, sadly. Not many people have, I guess. But this new one could change all that.

He had some of the titles right, almost everything else, including the plot of *The Old Man*, dead wrong.

You wouldn't happen to have any paper, would you? he asked as

Bailey and I were leaving. Thought I might take advantage of this, try to get some work done on the new book while I'm here.

I said I thought that was a good idea. Gave him the notebook and pen I always carried.

When I finished telling him about it, Walsh was silent.

"Damn, Lew," he finally said. "That's just plain creepy, any way you look at it."

I told him it definitely was, and he said he'd get back to me as soon as anything came in on the prints or photo.

I was lying on the bed, dipping in and out of dreams and thinking how any minute I was going to get up and put on coffee or maybe start a new career as a test pilot, when the phone rang again. Richard Garces, to tell me that, while the first responses to his request for information on the network were coming in, nothing thus far seemed to merit a closer look. I repeated my update on the hospital situation. He was appropriately incredulous.

"I have that list of local missions and community service centers you asked for. I don't suppose it's possible for me to just zap this over to you by modem."

"Not if you want it to get here."

"And still no fax, right?"

"Nope."

"Wouldn't you know it. And here I am fresh out of carrier pigeons."

"I'll swing by, pick it up."

After I'd done so, my first stop was on the stub end of Dryades, just before Howard breaks everything off into downtown streets. Forty years ago the building had probably been one of the big chain stores, a Montgomery Ward, a Sears; now, painted bright blue, it was the New Orleans Mission. Not without difficulty I found someone who finally admitted that well, yes, he did kind of look after things.

"You live here, then?"

He nodded. The only hair he still had was two thin patches, a couple of inches wide, above his ears. These hadn't been cut in recent memory and looked like limp wings. "Room downstairs, in the back, too small for much else. I sweep the place, clean toilets, lock up at night. They give me the room and meals."

I asked if the mission passed out clothes.

"Sure do, when we have 'em. Ever' so often a bunch of stuff'll turn up that somebody's give us. Don't never last long, though. Goes real quick. And then it's likely to be a spell before any more comes our way."

I asked about books.

"We got a few. Got 'em when the flea market up the street shut down, I think, year or so back. Can't say anybody's ever had much interest. They're stacked up down by my room still. Bible's 'bout the only thing anyone 'round here ever reads."

I showed him a picture of David and a copy of the one Don took of the patient claiming to be me and asked if he remembered seeing either of these men. He shook his head and, in exchange for a twenty, agreed to show me around.

Next stop was the warehouse district, until recently a desolate region of abandoned, boarded-up buildings and shattered sidewalks, now quickly filling with art galleries and upscale apartments built into the old hulls. The mission had no name beyond Gold Dew worked into the bricks above the doors, for the beer long ago brewed here.

A peculiarly small man sat at a desk to match in what was once the building's lobby. He wore a brown plaid suit with a bright yellow rayon shirt and blue knit tie that, from the look of the knot, never got untied.

"Hep you?"

I introduced myself and was telling him why I was there, when he interrupted.

"Look, you don't mind my saying, we got two int'rests, them that needs hep and those that's got somethin' for us to hep *with*. You dressed too good for the first, and 'less I'm mistaken I don't see you carryin' thing one. Have a nice day." He looked behind me. *"Next."*

No one there, of course.

Putting my hands on the desk, I leaned over him. If rain had broken out among the ceiling's high struts and girders, he'd have stayed dry.

He looked up, thought about it, and decided he might have time to hep me after all.

But he couldn't remember ever seeing either of those two. Couldn't be sure, of course, so many coming and going every day, so many that just needed a meal, a warm coat or a pair of shoes that didn't leak too bad.

I knew: none of them amounting to much more than their need.

We touched base on clothing and books, how the place operated, hours and occupancy, records. He'd think about it, get back to me should something come to mind. In the meantime maybe I had a dollar or two? Not for himself, mind you.

I gave him two twenties and stepped out onto the street. This part of town, it could still be 1940. The ancient brick buildings fill whole blocks, shut off view of the rest of the city: downtown's high-rise hotels, the Superdome. Trucks delivering foodstuffs, bread, beer, liquor and cleaning supplies thunder by. There's only the sky you see directly above you, this heavy, rumbling commerce, an occasional glimpse (high between buildings as you cross a street) of the twin-span bridge vaulting the river to Gretna and Algiers.

I crossed Canal, which not too many years ago was itself on the way to becoming a wasteland, and stopped at the Café du Monde for what remains the best cup of coffee in a coffee-crazed city.

The usual gaggle of tourists, dark-eyed locals and Quarter freaks, all in ill-fitting clothes. Tabletops and floor sticky as ever from powdered sugar. Cringeful out-of-tune calliope music from behind the levee, one of the cruise ships there.

A Swamp Tours van stopped out front to retrieve dropped-off clients, backing up traffic for blocks. Across by Jackson Square, carriage mules shrugged shoulders in their livery, flicked tails and snorted. A young man bantered at passersby on the sidewalk outside, periodically breaking off to perform solo versions of a cappella hits.

I had told myself that I wouldn't spend more than half the day trying to track down Lew Griffin₂. Then I'd get on with what I *should* be doing: looking for Shon Delany. Though really I shouldn't be doing either. I should be sitting at home getting notes together for my classes, possibly taking another look at the pages I'd done for what might be (increasingly I thought of it as such) a new book. I asked the woman at the next table if she had the time. For what? she said, then laughed and told me. Almost eleven. Okay. Thirty, forty minutes to walk there, another twenty to have a look around, I'd give myself that. Say one o'clock at the latest. Then I'd get back uptown, stop hunting snipe.

The next mission on my list lay well beyond the Quarter, on Derbigny out near Elysian Fields, a formidable hike. I had another cup of coffee to fortify myself.

They didn't know it, neither did I, but three guys hanging out at a corner store same as every day, wearing oversize jeans and backwards baseball caps, were waiting for me out there, along with a brushup on my arithmetic.

That's how life happens: angles, sharp turns, snags. Never what we expect. Never the stories we tell ourselves ahead of time. So we're always having to make up new ones.

8

I COULD HEAR Bat chiding me from just inside as I unlocked the door. Obviously much was amiss. I was a great disappointment to him.

One morning maybe six years before, he had shown up on Clare Fellman's screen door, claws anchored in the mesh, hanging there. She shooed him down and away but he kept coming back, till finally she let him in. He was little more than a kitten then, mostly skin and bone, with just these huge ears sticking straight up—which was how he got the name.

I'd kind of showed up on Clare's doorstep, too. And when I wouldn't go away, she let me stay.

We'd had a little over a year together, fourteen months almost to the day. With Clare, I'd been able for the first time to say things that, before, I'd always waited too long, too late, to say.

Then one night I came in and found her lying on the couch.

The night before, we'd attended a performance of the Kumbuka African Drum & Dance Collective at Loyola's Roussel Hall. Women meet to go about their daily work, scrubbing clothes, preparing food. One stays behind when night begins to fall and the others depart. Shortly she is set upon by a faceless demon. The others return and find her body. Their wailing and lamentations weave together into a hard rhythm that's finally picked up, almost unheard at first, by drums offstage. The women begin to dance as, slowly, the drummers come into sight—as together, ever more frantic, they drum and dance the woman back to life.

In the time we'd been together, Clare had discovered a flair for writing, and an unsuspected joy in it. The words that came to her so reluctantly, so haltingly, when she spoke, poured out in a flow when she wrote. She had started off writing op-ed pieces; soon she was doing reviews for local alternative papers.

I knew she was supposed to write up last night's performance and that it was due at *The Griot*'s office by six. Furthermore, this was Wednesday, her early day at school, so she'd been home since noon. But the only thing on the computer screen was the ensemble's name, below that the date and time of performance. Two spaces down, indented, the cursor blinked. A stack of students' papers sat untouched on the kitchen table where she usually worked.

I just don't feel very good, she told me when I asked what was wrong. I . . . feel . . . really bad . . . Lew . . . you know . . . ?

I'd been with her so long that I no longer noticed the pauses, the gropings, the way she drew lines around a word and waited for it to settle in place.

Come on, we're going to Touro, I told her.

Somehow I even managed to drive her car there. Because it was specially outfitted, with brake, gearshift and accelerator on the steering column, I'd never tried before.

In ER I raised enough hell to get her seen immediately. Neither the residents nor the attendings I insisted upon their calling in could find anything wrong. They suggested, nonetheless, that Clare remain overnight for observation.

I'd gone home to pick up a few things for her, pajamas and robe, toothbrush, underwear, makeup, her purse. Back in thirty minutes, I told her.

I knew something was wrong the minute I stepped inside the ER doors. People were rushing into Clare's room from all over.

Another cerebral aneurysm, I was told minutes later. Like the one that hit her when she was twenty-two, the one she wasn't supposed to survive, that scrambled her speech and caused her to have to learn all over again how to stand, walk, reach for things, grasp them.

Massive and sudden, a doctor said. Nothing they could do. They tried, of course. But . . . She was sorry.

So I moved out of Clare's, back again into the old house where I'd lived with LaVerne, taking Bat along. Where often I would stand looking out the window above the kitchen sink to the slave quarters, to the makeshift, long-forsaken office out there, its roof covered with grass.

Hours earlier, as I stood over a body I thought might be Shon Delany's, I'd been thinking about Clare.

I opened a can of tuna, real tuna, *people*'s tuna, and put it on the floor by Bat's dish. Rattled the feeder to shake down more dry food. Filled his bowl with fresh water.

Maybe I wasn't so bad after all.

I put on water for myself, set out a cup and a bag of Irish Breakfast tea, began rummaging through mail.

Cut-rate and presorted first-class advertisements from book clubs, record clubs, video clubs. An offer to provide me with a subscription to a catalog of catalogs. A refund check from the electric company for fifty-nine cents.

The kettle called, and Bat followed me back into the kitchen, thinking something more by way of food might happen there. Hope springs eternal. People drop things. The alert cat pounces before Providence has a chance to withdraw its offer.

That afternoon I myself had decided that Life, Providence, Chance or Whatever just might be sending me a message and, following the scuffle on Derbigny, returned home to shower off blood, grime and stray bits of skin and street tar, eat cold Dinty Moore beef stew out of a can, put on new clothes and head back out in pursuit of Shon Delany.

Signals we are set here to read. You must learn to put your distress signals in code. Move along, Griffin.

I did.

On foot, to the donut shop where Shon Delany had worked. By then it was almost four. And by then the shop was closed.

Not just closed. They'd pulled the rug out from under it. Tast-T Donut was shut down like a clam. Gone, abandoned, deserted, defunct.

A hand-lettered cardboard sign on the door read Sorry Were Not Here. The parking lot was full—employees' cars from the hospital and surrounding medical facilities.

Next door was a florist's shop. Stucco, a converted single-family residence with diminutive arches out front, every bit as charming as they were nonsensical. Recently painted light green and peach.

A bell tolled as I ducked through the entryway and came up against a trestle table behind which stood a woman at least six feet tall. Red hair everywhere, thin, wearing a black sheath. She was on the phone and, though motionless, somehow gave the impression of swaying. Willowy. She nodded to me, smiled. Be right with me.

"Yes, ma'am, I understand that. But if you could just come by the store? We'd be able to do a lot better job for you then. . . . Great."

She put the phone down. Bare arms slim and lightly downed. Wrists narrow as a ruler, fingers long when she reached across the table to shake my hand. Late thirties? No perfume, but a smell of soap and, behind that, the faintest trace of sweat.

Her earrings were tiny sharks with the lower halves of men's bodies hanging from their mouths.

"One problem working here is, a good-looking man comes in, I know there's no way he's bringing *me* flowers."

The phone rang again.

She shrugged. "Let the machine get it. People don't bother anymore even to bestir themselves."

Bestir themselves?

"They call from home in their pajamas or underwear and expect you to drop everything. Deborah O'Neil," she said, taking away her hand. "What can I do for you?"

She smiled, instinctively turning her head a few degrees to the side and lifting her chin. Incredible profile.

I asked her about the donut shop.

"Didn't *think* you looked like a flower man," she said.

She told me they'd been teetering at the edge (yes, she actually said *teetering*) for months over there. Some days they'd just put out on the shelves whatever was left over from the day before. Even the coffee got undrinkable. Not much for cleaning up, either, near the end. Counters so sticky you put your arm on one you have to shrug off your shirt and leave it there. Glued down for good. Only way they managed to stay afloat at all, long as they did, was by hiring new people when they couldn't pay old ones and let them go.

I said she seemed to know a lot about the situation over there, an amazing amount really, and she shrugged.

"I watch people, notice what happens around me. Always have. Things get slow here off and on during the day, you understand; it all comes in waves. And our office in the back has a window onto the alley. Employees take, took, their smoke breaks out there. I'd be doing the books, shuffling through piles of sales slips and invoices, and I'd hear them talking."

Did they know what was going on?

"They knew *something* was. The shop had recently been sold. Previous owner'd lost interest a long time back, and the shop just went on running itself, heading down the road the way it was pointed. New owner bought it as an investment, you see how it's all building up around here. He could care less about donuts. But the shop still went lurching along."

Any idea what finally shut the doors?

"Well, I don't know, of course. But I think it may have been what happened last night."

The phone rang again. Low voices from the back of the shop as the answering machine took the call.

"End of the month. Extra loads of paperwork to catch up on—even more, now that my partner never seems to be around for these things anymore. I've gotten used to being here late. Store closes at six, I'll get dinner and a glass of wine up the street at Sweet Basil's then come back and have two or three uninterrupted hours. So it must have been close to ten, maybe a little past. I was getting ready to leave."

This is last night.

"Right. I hear voices in the alley, someone saying 'Motherfuck,' someone else saying 'Be still, girl, don't you move or talk no more.' So I look out. This huge black car, Lincoln, something like that, 's pulled up out front. Four guys in it, all of them in black, too. And black. Driver stays in the car. The three that get out have automatic weapons. One stands by the car, watching up and down the street. Other two go inside. They're in there four, five minutes, come back out and get in the car. When the car pulls onto Jackson, people start running out of the donut shop. Lights are still on inside, but no one's there. This morning when I come in, I see the sign."

Robbery, you think?

"Who'd bother? Best day it ever had, that shop never netted two hundred dollars."

This town, it could happen. A few weeks back, an eleven-year-old knocked off a motel over on Claiborne. Walked in with a .38, pistol-whipped the desk clerk (though he had to get up on a chair to do it), and walked out with eighteen dollars. Still, she had a point.

You never saw anything like that before?

She shook her head.

They were looking for someone.

"That's the only thing that makes sense, yes. Way they went about it, the weapons, car."

Who was it in the alley?

"I don't know names. Just voices."

But you looked out, through the window?

"Yes."

You saw them?

"Not the woman. She was at the back, in the shadows. I remember the man sounded black but wasn't—that surprised me, when I saw him. Average height, fairly thin. Hair shaved to above his ears, then really long. Kind of a topknot. Like Woody Woodpecker?"

I asked her if by any chance she knew who owned the shop.

"Oddly enough, I do. He came by and asked if I'd mind keeping an eye on the property, maybe pass along any inquiries from prospective buyers. I have his name and phone number back in the office, if you want it."

I did.

"Assuming I can find it."

Which she did, finally: thumbtacked to the wall above the phone in a slurry of torn theater tickets, scribbled-over business cards, Post-it Notes, postcard announcements of gallery openings, panel discussions and seminars, posters and playbills for productions of *Endgame, King Lear and something titled Jimmy Baldwin Disembarks for Heaven.*

"You're in luck," she said.

I guess we both are.

"How so?"

Well, I see you got your play staged, for one thing, gesturing towards the *Jimmy Baldwin* playbill. What, a couple of months ago?

"No. That was last year."

It do okay?

"If you consider a week's run and half the house empty the whole time, it did. Actually I guess attendance was fairly good the first night or two. It gave a false impression. Because of family and friends."

You have a lot of friends?

The phone rang. Watching one another, we listened to her voice.

Heard the beep, heard a mumbled message, heard a dial tone as the caller hung up.

"Not so many that I can't use another one. But what's the second thing?"

What?

"You said we were both lucky because I got my play staged—for one thing."

You're right. Other thing was, I really do need to get some flowers.

"I see. What kind?"

Well, I was thinking roses. Pink if you have them.

"Of course. A dozen?"

Why not.

"I'll even pick them out myself."

She disappeared into the back room and emerged minutes later cradling thirteen baby-pink roses and sprays of baby's breath in green wrapping paper.

"And how would you like to pay for this, sir?"

Cash okay?

She punched it in on the computer (I heard a printer start up in back) and told me that would be $9.98. I pushed a ten across the breast-high table. She went back and got a copy of the printout for me.

"You'd like these delivered to what address, sir?"

Oh, you don't have to deliver them, I said.

She looked up. "I'm sorry?"

They're for you.

9

WE LIVE METAPHORICALLY, striving always to match our lives to images we've accepted or imagined for them—family man, middle American, true believer, gangster—contriving these containers, a succession of them, that preserve us, define us, that keep us from spilling out and give us shape, but rarely fit.

Kendall Gibbs lived this way more than most: everything about him expressed itself in relationship to one piece of land or another.

Using the number Deborah O'Neil gave me, I first tried to reach him at what was apparently an office. A woman answered "White House Properties," and when I asked for Mr. Gibbs inquired, "This was in regard to a listed, or a potential, property?" *Listed* and *potential* instead of selling and buying. Pure class. Admitting that Mr. Gibbs was out of the office (her tone implying that he was rarely, perhaps never, *in* the office), she suggested that I try another number, which proved to be a Garden District tour service. There, they thought Gibbs was out looking at a commercial plot on Bayou St. John, after which, to the best of their knowledge, he had no further appointments.

Once again I explained my interest: that I was handling a missing-persons case and needed to speak with Mr. Gibbs in regard to a recent acquisition, a donut shop at Jackson and Prytania. Former donut shop. I never implied any connection with the police, but the young man to whom I spoke assumed police business and, being *authorized* to do so, at his discretion, in such cases (ends of words neatly tucked under, a moment's pause before any new sentence began), decided he could give me Mr. Gibbs's beeper number.

I punched it in and within the quarter-hour had The Man himself calling from what sounded like a very busy street.

"Kendallgibbs," he said. All one word.

I told him who I was, what I wanted.

"I got a brother on the force, you know, fourteen years. Gerard Gibbs? Last four or five of them behind a desk. Light went out on Poydras, he's doing emergency traffic direction and gets run down by a drunk never even noticed he hit him. Worst job in the world. They put a muzzle on you, draw targets on your chest and Kick Me signs on your backside, scatter birdseed around you for pay."

I grunted what I hoped he'd take as assent.

"Okay. I'm away from my computer now, so I don't have access to files, paperwork. Of course, being a little old-fashioned, I do still manage to keep a thing or two in my head. What you want's not too complicated, I can probably help you."

"Thing I need most is to get in touch with the manager."

"There's not one. Assistant manager'd be the one you'd want. Manager walked out over a year ago. People who own the place think, Why pay someone to manage when this assistant's already doing it for scut wages."

"Guy with Woody Woodpecker hair?"

"Yeah, that's him all right. Keep expecting him to go Ha-ha-ha-*ha*-ha. Hard worker, though. Boy *was* the damn store. He hired, rode herd, ran totals and made daily bank drops, did more than half the baking himself, cleaned up when he could. I'm keeping him in mind, something comes up. Keith LeRoy."

"Then you have an address for him."

"Near's I know, no one does. Wouldn't give out an address, phone number. Boy plays it close to the chest."

Portrait of the middle-aged detective as Elmer Fudd running headlong into a wall. Staggering back arock on his heels.

"Well, is there anything—"

"I didn't say I couldn't help you, Griffin. You want his beeper, or E-mail?"

Beeper or E-mail. Guy's twenty years old, ran a donut shop for minimum wage, and he's got a beeper? E-mail? The world was getting away from me at an alarming rate. Sometimes I forgot.

Gibbs gave me both and I thanked him. He said no problem. Any-time.

"Yo," a voice said on the phone five minutes after I beeped.

"Keith LeRoy?"

"What chu want wit'im?"

I told him briefly, reminded him that we'd met three days back at Tast-T Donut.

He interrupted me, gliding back from street talk to standard. "I remember. Big guy, black suit—looked like linen—gold silk shirt. You still looking for Shon?"

"Yes." Four days in a row now, off and on. I was setting personal records for dogged persistence.

"Good to have some continuity in your life. Excuse me." I heard two voices speaking, one quarrelsome, the other flat and uninflected, just out of range of intelligibility. Neither sounded like LeRoy's. Then he said something and the voices stopped. "Sorry. I don't know what good this will do you, if any at all, but you're welcome to it."

"Whatever it is, it has to be better than what I have now."

"Yeah. Way we live, here in this great land. Okay. Last few times I saw him, Delany was hanging with a guy. Thought he was a friend, I'm sure— Delany didn't have any others—but the guy had that look in his eye, throw you over for a dollar?"

"You ever get his name?"

"Never came up. He'd just show up, wait outside for Delany to get off. Leaning against a wall, sitting on a customer's car. I asked Delany who he was once and he said that's my cousin. I told him tell his cousin to stay off the customers' cars from now on."

"That it?"

"Warned you it was thin."

"Then I'll try fattening it up. You have my thanks."

"And you have my you're-welcomes. *Damn* ain't we a couple of well-bred, civilized types."

"Who would have thought it?"

"Not *my* mother, for sure. Later, Griffin."

I sat looking at the envelope Sam Delany had given me, at the phone numbers printed on it, on the back flap, in precise, squarish figures. Nine times out of ten, the one thing they don't tell you is the very thing you need to know, the thing that would have kept you from running around in circles, into walls, dead ends and, often as not, trouble.

I dialed the number for Delany's rented room, then, glancing up at the clock, his mother's. He'd said he took care of the family. Maybe that included watching the younger kids after school.

"Baldwin-Delany residence." The eight-year-old, from the sound of it.

"Could I speak to Sam Delany?" I said.

"May I ask who's calling?"

I told her.

"I'll see if he's in."

He was, and was on the phone in the time it took to hand the receiver over.

"Mr. Griffin. Thank you for calling. You have news?"

"Nothing substantial." I told him about the donut shop closing, briefly recounted my conversations at the florist's next door and with Keith LeRoy. "Reason I'm calling is to ask if you know anything about a cousin of Shon's, guy he's been seen with lately."

"How lately?"

I said I wasn't sure. Couple of weeks maybe.

"And someone told you this was Shon's cousin?"

"That's how Shon identified him to the assistant manager at the donut shop, yes. Sounded like they might be tight. Getting that way, anyhow."

"Did you get a name?"

"No."

Moments went by. I could hear a TV in the background. X-Men, Ninja Turtles, something on that order. Kids' voices.

"I was afraid of that."

"So afraid that you didn't bother to tell me about it."

"I guess I thought if I said it aloud, somehow that was going to make it true. Like the kids when they were younger. They'd be in bed at night and think they saw something in the corner, so they'd be very careful not to look that way. Because if they did, it was going to be there."

"So who's this cousin?"

"His name's Armantine Rauch, everyone calls him Army. And he's not a cousin, he's Shon's half brother—like I am. One of Shon's old man's *other* adventures."

"You know him?"

"Much to my displeasure and misfortune, I do. Years back, Army showed up on our doorstep saying he had no other place to go. I was about Shon's age then—fifteen, sixteen. Mom's a pushover, as always. Has no idea how she's going to take care of the kids she already has but never even skips a beat before taking in this new one."

"How long was he with you?"

"Less than a year. First, money started disappearing from the coffee can in the kitchen, then from Mom's purse. Never *much* money, mind you, because there *wasn't* much. Fifty cents here, a dollar. Then we heard neighbors start complaining. Mail was missing from their box, they'd say. A grill or a lawn chair left on the gallery had disappeared. One man said the gallon of gas he'd put in his moped the night before, to get to work on, was gone when he went out the next morning 'round five. Few days later, a car got stolen from up the street. Not long after, police came knocking at the door. Wanted to know if an Armantine Rauch lived there."

"This had happened before, then."

"Every place he lived."

"It's the kind of thing that usually escalates."

"Did here too. Cops came by more than once, those last months. But then on one of the rare days Armantine actually went to school a teacher told him to do something he didn't feel much like doing and wound up with a pair of scissors in his chest. Kids said you could hear the air gushing out around them whenever the teacher, Mr. Sacher was his name, tried to talk, tell someone to please go get help."

"Rauch get tried for that?"

"After about fifteen social workers and agencies and this-n-thats you never heard of or saw before quit arguing, he did. Mama said we'd probably never see him again. Too goddamn bad. She used to visit, the first year or so, but it got to be way too hard on her and she stopped going. Funny. Maybe some ways, all that's why I'm in law school." He paused. "Almost in law school."

"He was tried as a juvenile?"

"Yes. Sentenced to twenty years, but they told us he'd be out when he hit twenty-one."

"And you haven't seen him since then, right? He didn't turn up at your mother's, you had no reason to think Shon might have taken up with him."

"Not really. Just that thinking about it, Shon disappearing that way, then finding out how things'd started changing on him and how none of us knew that, it gave me a bad feeling. Made me wonder."

"Okay, for the time being I guess that's it. Unless you have something else you forgot to tell me."

"No. I'm sorry."

"I'll get back to you."

"What—" he began.

But I hung up and immediately dialed Don.

"What's the name again?" he said after I briefed him. "This is local, right? We know where this kid was? Just a minute. Damn computer's just sitting here blinking at me."

Too many people surfing on the Third Wave.

"I'm waiting . . . waiting . . . I said *later*," he told someone. "Here it is. Armantine 'Army' or 'R. M.' Rauch. Went up on attempted second-degree, twenty to thirty. Remanded to LTI by judicial order. That's Louisiana Training Institute, and I've no doubt he *was* trained there, though not quite the way society intended. On the street they call it going to college."

"Plea-bargained?"

"Couldn't. They'd have tried to kick it down to manslaughter, even aggravated assault, but statutes say if the wound's to trunk or head it's gotta be second-degree. Evidence of past offenses, the usual escalation, was also entered."

"He's out?"

"Nineteenth of August. Happy birthday."

"Just like that."

"Yeah, butterfly time. The weird thing is, we have an address. I guess Rauch was carrying on an extensive correspondence while he was in prison, wanted to be sure it got continued once he was outside."

I climbed out of the cab in front of a tract house just across the parish line off Old Metairie Road. Almost certainly it had been military housing, later converted to fifties sub-suburban with accrual of screened-in porch, cinder-block utility room and partial second floor. Plywood nailed to the windows signaled a more recent conversion to abandoned building. The yard was ankle deep in rotting leaves, bright green clover, grenadelike pinecones.

Don's address had taken me to a poolroom-lounge on Jefferson Highway. The owner-bartender didn't appreciate my questions near as much as he had my business when I first came in and ordered a beer, and the whole thing quickly developed into one of those standard dialogues involving baseball bats produced from beneath the bar and bodies hauled across the top of it, after which he decided maybe it would be okay to tell me where R. M. was staying.

The front door gave with a sharp tug, nails pulling free of well-worn holes. Inside I found hard evidence of habitation: hot plate, pans, stack of dishes, aluminum percolator, canned goods, large tin of coffee, clothes that smelled of sweat hanging from nails in the wall. A plastic ice chest with two beer cans half afloat in tepid water and a pile of empty, crushed ones nearby.

In one corner, tucked under a sleeping bag, I found torn envelopes addressed to Armantine Rauch and letters beginning *Dear Arm*.

In another room I found, jammed into the wall behind broken paneling and swaddled in a canvas backpack, a long-barreled .22 target pistol.

In the last room I found a body lying facedown.

10

FOR SOME TIME words had been dropping without apparent reason or provocation, refusing to be dislodged, into my mind. Once it was *poshlost*, another time *sere*. Often these were words whose meanings I knew, if at all, imperfectly, though they were familiar.

Coming upon the body was like that. It wasn't Shon Delany's, but for a moment, for no good reason, I became absolutely certain that it was, and couldn't shake the impression.

I spent a couple of hours at the sheriff's office out there. In Jefferson Parish, unlike Orleans, it's the sheriff who handles police work. Officers sat across tables from me staring and served me plastic cups of coffee foul enough to elicit confession from the staunchest wrongdoer. They refused to get too worked up over this. Their attitude told me it was the kind of death that belonged to New Orleans, just happened to stray over the line into their territory.

I gave my statement, survived coffee and stares and when they finally agreed to put a call through, spoke to Don Walsh.

"Lew," he said, "I've been giving this some thought. What you need to work on is finding *live* bodies for a change. Maybe even the ones you're actually looking for."

"Good point."

"Let me talk to whoever's running the show."

His brief conversation gained my release and a ride home in one of the patrol cars. Nor did they make me drink any more coffee.

A note from Norm Marcus pushed under my door told me the kids on bikes had struck again, snatching a seventy-year-old woman's purse and pushing her off the curb. Her leg snapped when she went down. She'd managed to drag herself back up out of the street but had to lie there until someone driving by stopped to help her.

Having then fed Bat and drunk two cups of scalding tea in the rocker by the window that early Friday morning, I was still thinking of the body, and of Clare. I remember that I had every intention of getting up soon to fix myself something to eat.

I was thinking of that abandoned house in Metairie, how Armantine Rauch and others had been camping out there, as though it were only a shelter among trees; thinking how at every turn I seemed to keep running into people who were camping out, people living temporary lives. Maybe that's what we all do, ultimately. Remembering my own succession of apartments and houses. Thinking how even here, after all these years (neglectfully, I would have argued, though at some deeper level, I knew, willfully), I'd never filled in the blanks, never installed things in any kind of permanent place. Furniture, personal goods, books and papers remained where they were first put down; from appearance, I might just as well have moved in last week.

I was thinking, too, as I rarely did, of my mother.

Growing up, I never realized that all families were not like ours. My mother had withdrawn from the world, walled herself (as though Calvinist rather than Senegambian blood flowed in her veins) within exacting rituals of breakfast, job, dinner, housework, church, sleep. Whenever anything threatened or disturbed that routine, the very ground around us trembled. My father had chosen, if he had a choice, to withdraw alongside her. There were in our home no visits from parental friends, fellow workers, schoolmates. No family outings to movies, restaurants, the park. And no acknowledgment of my mother's silent, palpable madness.

Only years later did I begin to understand how strange and distorted that life was—distorted in ways no lens can ever correct—and how deeply scored by it I had been. It's a heritage my sister Francy seems largely to have escaped, though I've sometimes wondered if her own desperate grappling after normality, her sensible job, steady-keel husband and life, isn't in its way every bit as determined.

I was awakened, suddenly, by the phone. Foundering in bright light, confused. I pushed my way up and out of the rocker.

Children outside shouted to one another on their way to school. I had slept three, four hours. A peculiar grayness to the sky, as though seen through tinted glass. I didn't know it then, but a storage facility on Magazine had caught fire, pouring smoke into the uptown sky as cubicles of things people no longer needed but would not abandon, old letters and photographs and high-school yearbooks, wedding dresses, income-tax returns, crippled furniture, burned. Days later I watched a bulldozer crush and level what little remained.

As I stood there by the window, the machine took the call. This is Lew Griffin, please leave a message. Then Richard Garces's voice.

"Lew, ring me back when you get in. Your—"

I picked up.

"Richard. I'm here."

"Those bill collectors *will* be persistent, won't they?"

"Great, the driving-to-work comedy show. Ten minutes of bad jokes and three of even worse music."

He whistled a few notes and said, "You're an unreconstructed cynic, Griffin."

"I try."

"A sad and unhappy man."

"Indisputably."

"Okay, so I'm afraid I have further bad news for you," Richard said. "You ready for it?"

"I have a choice?"

"You're missing."

"I'm what?" I remembered Chandler's example of colorful American speech, a gangster ordering his subordinate from the room, saying simply: Be missing.

"Your guy over at University Hospital? The one that claims he's Lew Griffin? He's gone."

I watched a garbage truck lurch along the street outside. Men would jump off the back, grab a can, empty it and replace it at curbside almost in a single motion, then whistle the truck on, running behind. Fearful of loud noises, Bat was under the couch, ears at alert, eyes set hard on the front door.

"I have a friend who's a resident over there, knows you're a friend too. She called me when she heard about it. He went AWOL last night, sometime between about four and six."

"And no one saw him? Kind of hard to believe no one would notice, the shape he was in. I'm surprised he could even walk."

"Yeah. Everyone is. But people do the damnedest things all the time, things you never thought they'd be capable of."

Leaking fluids it was best not to think about, the garbage truck pulled around the corner.

"Anyhow, he'd been transferred to a room. He wouldn't have been, this soon, ordinarily, but I guess they needed ICU beds for casualties from a multiple pileup out on I-10.

"A nurse's aide checked vitals at twelve, two, and four. When the charge nurse herself went in for a final check at the end of the shift, six-twenty or so, she says, he was gone. His IV had been pulled out and was dripping onto the floor. There was a rubbery ball of adhesive tape in the sink. He took along toothpaste and toothbrush from a kit the hospital issues patients, left the razor and everything else behind.

"He also left his hospital gown, and no one could figure out what he did for clothes till later on, when another patient down the hall got back from X-ray. Someone had popped the lock on the suitcase in his room. Money and wallet untouched, but they took his clothes. Beige corduroy jeans, blue-and-yellow rugby shirt. Shoes gone too. Black Reeboks."

"You got all that from a friendly phone call?"

"Well, I asked a few questions. You know. I kind of had the idea you'd be going after him, Lew. That you could use whatever I was able to get you."

"I appreciate it, Richard, believe me."

I asked who his friend was at the hospital, wrote it down, and said I'd check in later.

Then I called Don, who told me he'd keep an ear open and added: "Damn, maybe it *is* you, Lew. Only man I know who's always out the hospital door before they can even slap tape on the bandages."

When I hung up, I saw the blinking light on the machine. I hadn't checked this morning when I came in.

The English department and Dean Treadwell would like me to call at my earliest convenience.

My agent had "small news and a smaller check" on a couple of foreign sales of old books.

Someone wanted to give me a free trial membership to a health club. And Deborah O'Neil wanted to thank me for the flowers.

I picked up the phone but, after a moment, put it down. I stood looking out the window, then got a pen and yellow legal pad from the shelf by the door and, returning to the rocker, wrote:

This was the first time I saw her. Wearing a red dress, she came in from the darkness. We were almost alone there in the small café.

Barely pausing, looking up only once or twice, I wrote for four hours.

11

SNOW.

Falling faintly and faintly falling.

Beginning Thursday afternoon as I headed home from the florist's on Prytania, continuing on into the evening as I sat remembering Clare's death, then through the night and into Friday morning as I sat by the window writing about LaVerne, temperatures had dropped like a kid cannonballing off a high dive: all impulse and plummet and loss of control, hard crash at the bottom.

Mention it to someone from New Orleans and he'll remember, to the moment, the times in his life it snowed.

January 1955. I was lead in the senior play and we had to cancel. Car went off the road into a drainage canal, this was up on Palmetto, other side of Carrollton, on my way home. Damn stuff was on the ground four days, shut the whole city down. It was pretty, though, I'll give you that—for about two hours.

February 1964. Sixty degrees and sunny on Friday, twenty-eight with a hard north wind that wouldn't quit by Saturday morning. Shutters banging against the house woke us up at five. Two days later, the snow started. It was getting towards Mardi Gras, I remember, everybody in a panic. But it did quit in time.

December, must have been 1971. Lot of snow—then a lot more ice. Second day, power lines went down, most of central New Orleans lost electricity. People were ripping the sides off of abandoned houses, setting them afire in fireplaces that hadn't been used for thirty, forty years. Firemen stayed busy that week.

"I only remember seeing snow one other time, all these years," Deborah O'Neil said across from me. She wore a long print skirt, sleeveless T-shirt and vest. I thought of my first impression: how, standing still behind the table, talking on the phone, she seemed to sway. Something substantial and at the same time strangely labile about her. "I'd been in town a week or so. That afternoon I was sitting out on the balcony with a cup of coffee, wrapped up in a blanket, trying to make some kind of sense of things, the husband I'd left behind in Florida, the man I'd moved here with, a night-shift job I hated, all these voices I kept hearing inside my head. They weren't talking to me, but they were definitely talking to someone.

"I looked around me there on the balcony, we were in one of three upstairs apartments carved out of an old house on Camp, and I realized it was snowing. Had been for some time. I watched snowflakes fall onto the blanket, or onto my jeans, jeans that had lasted longer than any relationship I'd ever had, and disappear, like they'd passed through walls. Others fell against the balcony railing, onto the leaves of a maple, into standing water at curbside. Into my coffee cup. The whole world glistened."

As it glistened now.

We sat across from one another watching snow fall, myself out the restaurant's front window, she in mirrors along the side, above tile. The waitress slid bowls of steaming gumbo off her tray, dropped a handful of packaged crackers between.

"And did you ever manage to make sense of things?"

For a moment she was silent.

"No. There was something about the snow, I don't know, but it made things, struggling to understand them, seem less important. Because whatever I did, whatever any of us did, that snow was going to go right on falling. . . ."

"On all the living and the dead."

She looked at me. "Yes. Exactly."

And scooping up a spoonful of soup, blew across it.

"That's what I thought the voices were for a long time. People who had died but were still around, who couldn't let go. I thought I was the only one able to hear them. Or that for some reason they could only get through to me—like I was the crystal in a homemade radio, wound with wires. Other times, I just thought I must be crazy."

Soup tipped from the side of the spoon into her mouth. "My God this is good! The green stuff's okra?"

"Ritual offering to the Slime God."

"The world, mind you, subscribed to the latter view exclusively."

"But obviously at some point you decided you weren't crazy."

She nodded.

"They really were ghosts, in a way, I suppose. People trying to speak, to come into being, through me. With time I learned that I could put them in plays, let them live *there*."

The after-work crowd began filtering in, pointedly snapping slouch hats against legs to shake off snow, slapping it away with hands from the shoulders of raincoats over business suits and office dresses. Typical city dwellers: were they really expected to put up with *this*, along with everything else?

A police station inhabited what was once a grand private dwelling across the street. State-of-the-art computer linkages within, battered Chrysler squads and scooters with blue lights on poles without. Patrolmen from over there in uniform and in jeans sat together, six of them, at a back table.

I had called and asked Deborah O'Neil if she'd like to meet me for dinner at Casamento's on Magazine, just off Napoleon. If she were free, that is, or could arrange it; I didn't know her schedule. She said sure, anyone who needed flowers that bad would just go up the street to Scheinuk's anyway, why not.

Menu and restaurant alike were fundamental. Not back to basics, because they'd never left: nothing about the place had changed in forty years. The menu, which like Eddie Lang's cues for the Whiteman orchestra could fit on a single index card, ran to oysters and shrimp: oysters on the half shell, oysters or shrimp fried, served up dressed or not on French or homemade bread, in stews and soups. You wanted vegetables, fries were available. The place itself was timeless pure New Orleans, one long room narrow as a boxcar and reaching to the street behind, kitchen hanging on the back like a caboose, floor and wall sheathed in tile, tables pushed close at either side.

"I'm glad you called," she said. "I didn't think you would."

Another spoonful of soup. Half a buttered cracker.

"I *hoped* you would."

The door opened again and cold air flooded in. Before long these front tables would be abandoned, everyone huddled away from them, farther in past the open archway. Cavelike in there. As the night came on.

"You left the man you moved here with, I take it."

"That same afternoon. I was sitting at the kitchen table with my bags packed when he got home from work. The snow hadn't stuck, but there was a thin layer of ice on everything. I remember how it broke on the steps as I went down them. I've lived alone ever since."

"How long?"

"Almost ten years. Though I have to think: my God, how is that possible? I was twenty when we moved here. Last month I turned thirty. What about you?"

Did I live alone? "Yes." Even when I was living *with* someone, if LaVerne had been right. And she was, about most things.

I told Deborah, briefly, about LaVerne. Maybe not so briefly.

"She sounds like an amazing woman."

"She was."

We talked on. About what I did and had done for a living all these years, about Vicky, about Jimmi Smith's murder and his sister Cherie's coming to live with Vicky and me, about Alouette and Baby Girl McTell.

Deborah asked if she could have a glass of wine, and I said of course, ordering coffee for myself.

"Well, whatever else it may have been, Lewis, you can never complain that your life's been boring."

She swirled wine about her glass, in a quick circle, twice.

"Legs," she said.

I looked at her over the rim of my cup.

"That's what they call those breaks of wine, the way they cling to the side of the glass, run down it. Legs."

A United cab pulled up out front and honked.

"So tell me, Detective Griffin. Are you on a manhunt tonight?"

"No," I said, looking about me. "No. I'm not."

12

THE MAN IN the white tuxedo and the woman in a black silk dress come walking out of the mouth of the mine that moments ago collapsed. Spumes of dust pour from the opening behind them. In this bright sun it looks like smoke. They are holding wineglasses, slim, fluted ones of crystal, through which the sunlight shatters into rainbows and projects itself onto hills, trees, clothing, faces.

Don Walsh's call at eight in the morning hauled me from the dream and informed me that the body I'd found out on Old Metairie Road belonged to one Daryl Anthony Payne, Dapper or Dap to his friends—from his initials and looks both, apparently. He was, or had been, a model, put himself through two years of school up at Tulane on what he made modeling clothes for mail-order catalogs, with plenty left over for a fancy apartment overlooking St. Charles, a vintage MG roadster and holidays in Mexico.

But then something happened. Something changed. You looked at his life, it was like reading a piece of paper held over a candle. Everything turning brown, burning through from the center, coming apart. All of a sudden there was never enough money. Payments on credit cards got later, smaller, while finance charges kicked them into overdrive. Rent got paid only on demand. NOPSI, the phone company, and Cox Cable monthly threatened to discontinue service if. And Daryl was out hustling jobs—TV commercials, trade shows— he wouldn't have touched with gloves on a year ago.

"Begin to look familiar?" Walsh said.

"Gambling or drugs. A second life."

"You got it."

Looking out the window, I remembered at some point during the night rousing sufficiently to kick away covers. Now the temperature continued to rise, as rapidly as yesterday and the day before it had dropped. Bright sun, a riot of bird calls. Japanese tulip trees soon would be in bloom. Each year they came first, lugging the scenery of spring onstage. Weeks later, azalea followed: squat, graceless bushes at roadside exploding into heaps of pink, white and fuchsia blossoms.

"We know of any connection between this guy and Armantine Rauch?"

"Nothing on paper. Payne was on the long slide down, though, no doubt about that. Maybe he just fetched up against Rauch somewhere along his way. Kind of thing that happens. There's a good chance Rauch was collecting part-time for one of our local sharks. Sounds to me like the kind of guy who'd get off on breaking an occasional finger. And that would fit in with both their patterns, Payne's *and* Rauch's. I touched base with our regular snitches, sent some pigeons out. I'll let you know what they bring back."

"Not likely to be olive branches, I guess."

"Not likely."

"Thanks, Don. I'll be in touch."

He made no reply, but the connection stayed open. Behind him I heard the usual noise and bustle. Ringing phones, raised voices. A steady low rumble, like the sea.

"Don?"

"Mmmm."

"There something else?"

"Nah, not really."

"Yeah. Well, seems like I remember someone standing over my hospital bed a while back telling me that whatever else I'd done, the one thing I never did was bullshit him. You remember that too?"

"Yeah. Yeah, sure I do. Remember a lot of things. Things I wish I didn't." I heard him sip noisily. From his purple, green and gold Mardi Gras mug that read *It's a bitch*, I figured. "Funny how so much of it just piles up on top of us, Lew."

Memory holds you down while regret and sorrow kick hell out of you: I'd written that in *The Old Man*.

"It's Danny. He wasn't there when I got home Wednesday night, and I haven't heard from him since."

I waited.

"Not the first time, of course. Not by a long shot."

"No."

"But you know that."

I knew. Just as I knew Don's pain. There wasn't much I could do about either.

"So what am I worried about, right?"

"Maybe things will work out, Don."

"Sure. I figure, give it another couple days. Then maybe I'll go looking. I have some time coming to me."

Walsh must have had *years* coming to him. He routinely worked double shifts, days off, weekends and holidays. The department had to threaten him with suspension just to get him to take his vacation.

"Comes down to it, maybe you'd go looking with me."

"No maybe about it, old friend. You know that."

"Later then, Lew. And thanks."

I hung up thinking how if you weren't careful life could turn into a long chain of laters, one after another, till one day you looked around and there was nothing left, no trace of all the things you'd waited for, pushed ahead, done without.

Too busy with their future to bring her presents, as a friend's poem put it.

I was on my way showerward (as, speaking of poets, Gerard Manley Hopkins or Dylan Thomas would say) when the phone rang again.

"Lewis? Deborah. I'm scrambling for work, running late, which I'm used to, but I wanted to tell you how much I enjoyed last night, which I'm *not* used to, and that I hope we'll get together again soon. Call me? Bye."

I stood listening to the dial tone. I hadn't said a word.

I dialed her home number and, when the machine shut up and let me, said, "Me too."

Then I put on coffee, along with a pan of milk to warm. Stood by the front window as I waited. Traffic falling off out there now. Three or four cars hurtle past at a time, then the street's empty, a kind of Morse. Housewives in sweaters to their knees with dogs on leashes emerge. Androgynous bicyclers in bright helmets and tights. Then from the kitchen the sound of the coffeemaker gulping through filter and grounds these last drafts of water. Almost forgot. Milk must be smoking, have a skin over it by now.

On the table nearby sat the legal pad I'd been writing in yesterday. Half a dozen empty scored pages remained. The rest were folded to the back. Lines thereon crowded with crossings-out, insertions. New passages written sideways in the margins, circled and arrowed in.

From her street corner, from her seat at some bar or in some hotel lobby, she watched that other city gather, rising out of the night as though from dark water. This was the place, the world, she knew best. Its names and faces, its appointments, its unspoken accommodations.

That afternoon she woke from a dream.

No.

With a moment's thought I struck *she* and scrawled above it *I*.

That afternoon I woke from a dream.

Obviously within some large city, but one neither of us knows on sight, we emerge from the subway. Winter—and breath-catchingly cold. Moonlight glances off ice and snow. Steam rolls from the exit behind us. There's no traffic, no one else on the streets, though in the occasional high window we see people still at work before desks and computer terminals.

We turn to one another. His black mask above a white tuxedo. My own white mask over a dress of black silk. Beneath these unearthly buzzing streetlights. Lewis's lips move without sound. I cannot make out what he is saying. I reach for him, my hand huge as a sky. His face recedes from me, like a train pulling slowly away.

When I was done, I went back through what I'd written before and changed it all to first person. Nowhere near the simple adjustment I'd thought: whole passages had to be recast, reimagined, rewritten.

I had no idea any longer what it was I might be writing—memoir, essay, biography, fiction. And as the book progressed in following weeks I grew forever less certain. But I found, as well, that I didn't care.

Often before, I'd written close to my life and at the same time from a distance. What was true, what was not true? or true, perhaps, in some sense having little to do with mimicry, fact, accurate tracings of our lives? There were deeper currents, deeper connections, surely. I fumbled after them.

As from the kitchen came the smell of burning milk.

13

DR. LOLA PARK stepped through the automatic doors from the OR in yellow scrubs and a tired smile, looked about, and headed straight for me. Blue paper covers on her shoes. I stood.

"Mr. Griffin. Richard called to say you'd be coming over. I don't know that I'm going to be much help to you, though. I can't even promise I'll make sense, at this point. I've been on call almost forty-eight hours."

We shook. Her hand was slender and strong, fingers unusually long and curving slightly back on themselves, nails cut close. Lots of blond hair pulled carelessly to the back of her head and pinned up. No trace of makeup, though maybe she'd started off with it two days ago.

"You and Richard are old friends," I said.

"Well, it did take a while for us to get that way again. But yes, we are."

I hung an expression of polite inquiry on my features, like putting a Be Right Back sign in a shop window. She responded with a smile, high cheekbones rising still higher.

"We were married, Richard and I. A long time ago. Neither of us much more than a kid then. I see you're surprised."

"All things considered, yes. I am."

"Well, so were we. What we had in common you could have put on a Post-it Note. God knows what we thought we were doing, or if we thought about it at all. It just kind of happened, there we were one day, my God, we're married. The biggest thing we shared was, back then we had the same taste in men—bad. And when I decided women were really what it was all about for me, we lost even that. Though we held on awhile still. Had some romantic image of ourselves as outlaws, I think. United by that. Pushing at the barricades. It all seemed quite daring at the time."

Her beeper sounded and she stepped to a phone on the wall by the OR doors to respond, was back within the minute.

"Anyway," she said. "Richard says you're trying to find yourself?"

"Aren't we all."

"Frankly, I don't think most of us ever even notice we're missing."

"I appreciate your seeing me, Dr. Park," I said.

"Lola. And believe me, seeing you is a welcome break. I spent the last forty-six hours peering into compound fractures, gunshot wounds and eviscerations, gaping mouths, vacant eyes. Most of the rest of the time looking out the window, wondering at exactly what point it was that I dropped out of anything resembling a real life."

"Can I buy you a coffee? Breakfast, maybe?"

"Breakfast would be nice. It'll have to be the cafeteria, though. Nothing down there you can recognize on sight. They have to put labels on it."

She reached down to push the button on the beeper clipped into her waistband. It gave off a single low-pitched squeal. She would do this repeatedly, in the middle of sentences, between gulps of coffee, the whole time we were together. I don't think she was even aware of it. This had become her connection to the world, her bridge. Instinctively she protected it.

"On into the belly of the whale, then. I warn you: you may want to leave a trail of bread crumbs. Or hack notches on the tunnel walls as we turn."

We took a phone booth–sized elevator to the third floor, crossed through an uneven, close passway ("That's the new part of the hospital back there," Lola told me, "now we're in the old") to a kind of enclosed platform where we had a choice of elevators, stairs or emergency exits, picked one from among the first and again went down, debarking into a narrow chamber.

Now we confronted a dozen or more steel doors, single, double, most askew in frames and lacking elemental hardware (screws, handle, hinge), none of them marked. We went through one, heard it slam and shudder into place behind us, into a maze of corridors where floors sloped ever downward and clusters of pipes and conduits paced our descent overhead.

At last we emerged into a long, cavelike room aflood with artificial light.

People sat slumped over trays of meat-and-two-vegetables, sandwiches assembled days before, prepackaged cookies, bags of chips and candy, ice cream bars. Plastic glasses of iced tea with lemon slices like small rising suns on the horizons of their rims. Waxed-cardboard cups of coffee. People themselves looking waxlike, plastic, and not at all like rising suns.

"Half a star for atmosphere," Lola said, "but the food's even worse."

"Then the stories are true. There *is* a whole population living down here beneath the city."

As I watched, sipping coffee, Lola devoured three fried eggs over easy, two servings of hash browns and another of buttered grits, order of bacon, wheat toast. No inordinate fear of cholesterol here. But she wasn't an internist, after all; she was a surgeon, with that mentality. Surgeons are technicians, sprinters. Friend of mine calls them slashers. Whatever the problem is, you just hack it off or out, sew the hole shut. Your basic Republican solution.

Twice her beeper sounded, and she went to the phone on the wall by the cashier to answer.

Twice she came back, said No problem and went on eating.

Third time, she said, Break's over, I guess. Nothing gold can stay. Couple of street soldiers up there losing ground fast.

Think I might be able to find my way up and out without help?

Probably so.

"Richard said you'd want this. It's got your name and phone number inside the front cover. Only thing left behind in the room. I snagged it off Housekeeping's cart. On its way to the elephant's graveyard, otherwise."

Pulling it from her lab coat—pockets bulging with stethoscope, hemostats, treatment regimens, a ruler to lay along EKG tracings, prescription forms—she handed me the notebook I'd left with our mysterious departed patient. I glanced quickly through it. Page after page, top to bottom, margin to margin, in a neat, close hand. Written straight out with almost no corrections.

Her beeper sounded again. She punched the button, knocked back the last of her coffee and stood.

"Richard said it was important to you. No problem. Things can get lost in the shuffle around here. Hell, *people* get lost in the shuffle around here."

"Thanks, Lola."

"For what?"

"For caring, I guess."

"Yeah. Well. I think I did at first, anyway. Now I talk to you down here, go back up there and save a life: what's the difference? I sew one guy's heart back together, another one's just going to roll in the door ten minutes later with an EMT's finger jammed into his ventricle."

"I'm not sure I believe that."

"That I don't care?"

I nodded.

"I'm sure you don't want to."

Her beeper sounded again. Insistent, shrill, this time. Simultaneously there came an overhead page: *Stat to ER-2, stat to ER-2. Code blue. Code blue.*

"We're all little Dutch boys, Lewis. And the dikes are giving way all around us."

She grinned.

"No pun intended."

14

THREE CALLS THAT morning, beginning as I came in the door from the hospital, points on a line pulling together discontinuous events and years.

"Lewis, that you, man?"

Since I had never heard his voice before, I didn't recognize it.

"I'm out."

So I said something noncommittal.

"They threw me out. Whoa, I told them. Wait a minute, I wanta see my lawyer. You *are* your lawyer, they said. Hard to defeat that kind of logic."

"Zeke?"

"The same. Well, *not* the same, truth be told. Actually, quite different right now. Gola's the only home I can remember, you know? *Damn* there's a lot of stuff going on all the time out here. Traffic shooting by, people walking straight at you from ever' which direction, shouting at each other from two blocks away. Some kind of siren screaming past ever' couple minutes. Always like this, huh?"

"Pretty much."

"You people could do with some peace and quiet."

"I'm sure we could. On the other hand, we can make a trip to the bathroom or eat a meal without getting a ground-down spoon handle shoved up our ribs."

"Lewis. Hey, I read the *Times-Picayune* first thing this morning, see 'bout the competition, find out what I'm getting myself into out here. Twenty-one murders in seven days, am I right? Way things look to me, most of the city, you so much as step out to get your mail you're taking your life in your hands."

"You're right."

"You know I am."

"And here you are now, out here with the rest and the best of us."

"Five hours, twenty-nine minutes and some-odd seconds. *Very* odd. Wearing this fine blue suit, hard shoes, worried look and the People of Louisiana's best wishes. *Damn* you got some fine women walking the streets. Good behavior, they told me back at Gola. Now, we *both* know better than that, don't we?"

"So what's going to happen to the paper?"

"Boy name of Hog taken it over. Worked with him some, boy could jus' be all right. *Way* past time for a change, everybody knew that. Last few years, you read the paper and you might as well be watching some rerun from nineteen sixty-two. Who the hell *are* these guys in leisure suits and these long-ass shirt collars up there, they look real to you? Old men ought to shut up once you done heard all their stories."

Ezekiel was my age. We'd "met" when I published *Mole*, a novel starting off with a killer's release from prison and going on to document the cobbling together and collapse of his life outside, and received a letter from the Louisiana State Penitentiary at Angola.

Ezekiel had been at Angola over thirty years then, since an attempted robbery went bad and left two employees gravely injured, a bystander dead. He was seventeen at the time.

Ezekiel had barely got through the fifth grade. But in prison he began to educate himself, first reading his way through the prison library, then writing to churches outside the prison asking that their members donate more books, which he also read, finally to university libraries to request any books pulled from their shelves. A college in southeastern Louisiana sent a cache of old editions of law books. Ezekiel holed up for over a year studying them.

Sometime in the seventies, when the new Supreme Court rulings came down carrying Zeke's death sentence along with them, to simple life, he took over editorship of the prison weekly, transforming it from a bulletin board for the prison administration to a real newspaper. Stories appeared on prison employees who purloined quality meats purchased in bulk for the prison, substituting hot dogs and cheap bologna; others documented a cruel, corrupt and hugely ineffective prison medical program. Threats came down from all sides. But support from reform-minded wardens and the wide attention Zeke's efforts had gained from national newspapers helped protect him.

He'd first written to tell me how much he liked *Mole*. Then every now and again he'd write to ask my advice about matters at the paper, and finally, though we'd never met, we'd put in enough time to become friends of a sort. I introduced him by mail to Hosie Straughter, who wound up picking up a lot of his stuff, columns and a half-dozen or so features, for *The Griot*.

Now Ezekiel was back out on streets *I* barely still recognized, so much had changed in recent years. And in thirty-three of them? It wasn't even the same world.

"What, they didn't warn you this was about to happen, discuss it with you?"

"Sure they did, Lewis. I just didn't believe them. Why *would* I, after all those years? How many times you think I heard how much better things were about to get?"

"So what are you going to do?"

"Well, I tell you. Right now I'm at a phone booth 'cross from Ruby's Fishhook Bar and Lounge trying to remember how a glass of cold beer tastes. I think, once I hang up, I'm gonna have to go in and find out. After that, who knows. See what life has to offer. You purely can't imagine how strange this all is, Lewis."

"You're right. I can't. And it doesn't matter how hard I try, how hard I want to."

"No." Behind his silence, clouds in a clear sky, I could hear sirens, raised voices, automobile horns. "But sometimes wanting to, trying to, is enough, Lewis. That's as close as we ever really get anyway, most of us."

"You have a place to stay?"

"State gave me a list, halfway houses and the like. Takes care of its own, you know."

"Yeah. Sure it does. Join our happy little family of guys lying awake all night flat on their backs staring at the ceiling and trying not to scream."

I told him my address.

"If I'm not here, the key'll be under a brick in the flower bed out front, one nearest the door. It's a big house. Stay as long as you need to, come and go as you want."

Silence again. "You sure about this, Lewis?"

I thought about Vicky years ago, asking Cherie to stay with us until she got her life together. Remembered before that, before he was killed, Cherie's brother Jimmi sitting up in the bed next to mine at the halfway house reading a book on economics. And how Verne's last years, past the shutters of her personal pain, were given over to others. She made a difference in a lot of lives around here, Richard Garces had told me.

"I'm sure," I said.

"Then maybe I'll be seeing you soon, huh. After all these years."

I'd barely hung up, had the thought I'd love a drink and triumphantly decided on coffee instead, wandering out to the kitchen to see about assembling some, when the phone rang again. I picked it up out there.

"Mr. Griffin?"

"Yes."

"You may not know my voice. A number of years have passed since we met."

"I know it."

"Yes. I suspected that you would, of course. I also suspect that you well may choose not to speak with me."

He waited without saying more.

"Go on."

"Thank you. This *is* quite difficult for me. Perhaps for both of us."

My turn to wait now.

"I will not apologize for our past encounters, Mr. Griffin."

"I would never have expected you to."

"Very well."

Wondering if I'd ever actually heard someone say *Very well* before, I watched a mouse ease out from beneath the refrigerator and inch along the baseboard. Part of its tail was missing.

Guidry, Dr. Guidry, was Alouette's father, the one who had pushed her mother away, sequestered Alouette from her. Just before she died, LaVerne had been trying to get in touch again with her daughter, at that time a runaway. And just *after* LaVerne died, because she would have wanted me to, I found Alouette up in Mississippi, only to have Guidry descend with well-dressed lawyers and threadbare threats. Alouette chose to come back with me to New Orleans, and for a while it looked as though things were going to work out for her—but I guess it had looked that way before. I came home one day and she was gone.

"I may have misjudged you, Mr. Griffin."

"You're not the first."

"It is possible, also, that you may have misjudged me."

The mouse had found the gap in the cabinet door under the sink and hoisted itself up and over.

I said nothing.

"I'm in touch with you now," he said shortly, "because some weeks back, I had a call from my daughter."

Frogs have been known to fall from the sky without warning. Pianos. Hailstones like fine crystal.

"It was, as you will understand no doubt, a terrible surprise, wholly unanticipated. Years have gone by. Years in which I have had no word from my daughter and, despite considerable efforts on my part and behalf, proved unable to learn even her whereabouts. I suppose, in fact, that I had come to resign myself to her continued absence—inasmuch as one ever does." He paused. "You're a father too, as I recall."

"Did she tell you where she was calling from?"

"No."

"Or why she was calling after all this time? Did she ask for money?"

"Perhaps she intended to. She would have gotten it, of course. Whatever she needed, without question. But very soon—we'd scarcely begun talking—we were cut off."

"Probably she just spooked, when it came down to it, and hung up."

"That is certainly possible, of course. But I think not."

Very well and *I think not*, both in the space of minutes.

"She said she was in trouble, Mr. Griffin."

"Trouble's pretty much where she lives. You know that."

"Which is why I have to think that, for her to call me, the trouble this time must be extraordinary. At any rate," he said after a moment, "it occurred to me that, whatever trouble she might be in, as long as she remained capable of doing so, you're the other person Alouette would be likely to contact." He cleared his throat. "Have you heard from my daughter, Mr. Griffin?"

"No. Neither recently, nor since she left here. I'm sorry."

"I see. And could I ask a favor? You've certainly no reason to grant me one, I realize."

"I'll call you if I hear from Alouette—yes."

"Thank you, Mr. Griffin," he said quietly. "Perhaps we might get together for lunch one day."

Moments went by.

Then the dial tone.

The third call came later, as I settled ever deeper into my old white wood rocker by the front window. Shutters pulled, blinds drawn. Murmur of a rising wind outside. I was on my third cup of coffee, playing a Mozart serenade for winds that was a favorite of Clare's.

I picked up the phone on the fifth ring and said hello.

Though no one answered, the line stayed open, and for whatever reason, I didn't speak again. I stood listening, feeling the presence there at the other end, on that other shore.

Then the dial tone.

In a drawer of my desk I had a seven-year-old tape with two twenty-second segments that sounded and felt exactly like this. Back then, not long after I pulled the cassette from my answering machine, sitting in darkness like a cat with the fruity smell of gin and a murmur of wind outside, I had known that the old man's bottle and mute acceptance in that final scene from my novel were my own, and that I would not see my son, would not see David, again.

15

I CAN TELL you in a few words who I am: lover of woman and language, in terror of the history whose responsibility I bear, a man awake at night and alone.

At 3:52 A.M., to be precise.

I put the book down and picked up, for the second or third time, my empty glass. The radio was on, Art Tatum silk-pursing some well-nibbled sow's ear of a popular song. Zeke had turned up around nine and now was installed, and asleep, upstairs. I could hear the window unit in his room laboring; whenever its compressor kicked in, lights dimmed momentarily, like a caught breath.

This time of night, this circle of light with music welling up outside, this solitude—we were all old friends. Over the years we'd sat here together many nights just this way. With houses and apartments empty around me, with Alouette asleep upstairs, with Vicky away at the hospital taking on the nightly freight of violence that finally sent her, low in the water, home to France.

Or with LaVerne out working. We'd climb from bed at five or six, when most of those caught up in the world outside our window (so very, very different from the world inside) were ending their day, to begin ours.

Suddenly Bat emerged from the darkness around me and sprang onto my lap.

Ezekiel had been something of a surprise too. Not long after I got back home, he'd come knocking at the door and when I opened it, said, "Lewis?" Peering up, because he topped out at about four foot six. "Here I am."

He looked not at all like any of the photos of him I'd seen. What he looked like was a cypress knee someone had carved into the likeness of a man.

I fed him leftover red beans and rice while we sat at the kitchen table going through a couple of pots of coffee together. Topics? How exciting and scary Zeke's first months at the prison paper were, and how uninspired the last years, when only a sense of duty and need of something to do kept him plodding doggedly on. Praise for Hosie Straughter's crusading work with *The Griot*—now published out in Metairie and given over exclusively to "arts and entertainment." Excited questions about movies like *Boyz N the Hood* and Spike Lee's, which of course he'd not seen. Mention of the novel Zeke thought he might someday write. Until finally he said, "Okay, Lewis. Point me to my corner. 'Cause this ol' fighter's 'bout to fall down."

High point of the afternoon had been when I dropped by Deborah's, about six, to say hello and make a date for dinner the next day. "You mean I'm getting asked out? Like normal people?" she said. I asked her if Commander's would be okay, and she told me it always had been. "But let's go early. Because afterwards, I have a surprise for you."

Low point of the afternoon was everything else.

Following that morning's three phone calls, I'd sketched out my itinerary: head uptown to see what I could find out about Daryl Anthony "Dap" or "Dapper" Payne at Tulane's registrar; revisit the tract house on Old Metairie Road where I'd come across the body and where surely some subtle, obtuse clue awaited me; along the way, check out outlying missions and shelters.

That was an awful lot of moving about.

I called Don back.

"You using your car?"

"What for? No way they're letting me leave here, not with all *this* shit going down. For all I know they've got it booted, so I *can't* get away."

"Okay if I borrow it?"

"Why not? It's in the lot out back. I'll send the keys down, let them know you're coming— Hang on, Lew, I've got another call, supposed to be urgent." He was gone four, five minutes. A couple of times other people came on, asking if they could help me, and I told them I was holding. Then Walsh was back.

"That was Danny, Lew. He's okay. Says he met an old friend at one of the malls, some guy he went to school with. Been staying over with him, catching up on old times. They saw a movie or two, had some burgers. He's home now. Said he'd probably sleep right through to tomorrow."

"That's good, Don."

"Yeah. So, you gonna bring the car back here when you're through with it, or what?"

"I'll bring it back."

Though for all the good it did me I might as well have left it there in the lot, and sat in it myself the whole time.

Yo, black sheep. Got any wool? I'm down for it, man. Three bags full.

And wool's all it was.

No one at Tulane could tell me anything I didn't know already. Out on Old Metairie Road a lawn mower had been run through the ankle-deep rotting leaves and sashes of yellow police tape clung to trees, but nothing else had changed. The two or three mission-looking places I found were closed—whether permanently or just for the day, I couldn't tell.

So around six, swimming upstream of outbound traffic, Middle America making its way home, I drove back into New Orleans, dropped by Deborah's to say hello and set up our date (parking illegally out front: most cops knew Don's god-awful old Regal by sight), and returned the car. Don and I had dinner together, my treat, at Felix's. Danny wasn't mentioned.

Then I'd come home by streetcar and, within minutes, answered the door to find Ezekiel peering up at me.

Once he was tucked in, I poured a Sharp's and settled down in the rocker to read, sleepy but still wired. I tried going back through what I'd written in the legal pad that morning but couldn't concentrate, couldn't stay afloat on it. Next I tried a small-press book I'd bought several months past, on pure impulse, at Maple Street. It had sat on the coffee table ever since, cover curling from humidity so that I'd kept turning it over, back to front and back again.

They come in the dark and do terrible things to me. They go away.

But I didn't do much better with that than I'd done with my own stuff.

I found myself thinking about the notebook Lola Park had given me at the hospital that morning.

I went over and got it from the breast pocket of the coat I'd hung on the back of the hallway chair.

I'd carried the notebook for over a year. It was about eight by four, the size of a large wallet and half the thickness of a deck of cards, tape binding pulled away in the middle from constant recontouring to pocket and body. Stitched pages, blue and white composition cover.

As with many good ideas, at first I'd used the notebook readily and often, before letting it slip into neglect. A dozen pages or so bore scribbled notes for classes and stories, snippets of overheard conversation, bits of description, the occasional address or phone number, errand lists, wobbly columns of Dewey decimal numbers copied from the school library's computerized catalog, lists of trees or of lawyers' and street names. Some of the notes were impenetrable, whatever import they once may have had now lost in the folds and trouser cuffs of time.

All of that had been entered the first month or so I carried the notebook around. The rest of the pages remained empty.

Now, though, they were filled—literally filled, top to bottom, left to right, had to be fifty, sixty lines to the page—with a tiny script that managed simultaneously to look like a continuous, unbroken line and put one in mind of cuneiform.

"My book. One of them," the accident victim, the man I'd first thought to be David, Lew Griffin$_2$, had said.

And what he'd done in this notebook I'd left him (I realized upon reading several pages) was recast *The Old Man* in diary form. The central situation, individual scenes, settings, dialogue: all were there. But so were elements that had nothing to do with my story—scenes and language that never belonged to it, never belonged *in* it, never would.

The notebook's unnamed, transparent diarist lives on the streets, moving freely through the city, watching people come and go and afterwards, in an attempt to understand them, making up stories about them: who they may be, how they pass their days or nights, what's important to them and what scorned, memories, dreams.

One day on Magazine he watches two men, the first older, white, the other a young black, leave a bar together, shake hands and strike out their separate ways. He thinks how very much, for all their visible differences, the two men resemble one another, self and shadow. And from that moment of unpresuming observation, the story—the note-book's remaining pages, its retelling of my novel—gains force and spins itself out.

When, years later, I met the younger man's son, it was with mutual, quiet recognition. You're David, I said.

Yes.

16

THE PAST IS no insubstantial, thready thing, sunlight slanting through shutters into cool rooms, pools and standards of mist adrift at roadside, memories that flutter from our hands the instant we open them. Rather is it all *too* substantial, bluntly physical, like a boulder or cement block growing ever denser, ever larger, there behind us, displacing and pushing us forward.

And yes: in its mindless, rocklike, solid, unstoppable way, it pursues us.

Once, I'd begun a short story comprised of a series of footnotes to another, undivulged text, footnotes that were to form among themselves a coherent, though discrete, text.

Another time I planned a novel each chapter of which would end midsentence, the next chapter scooping up the rest for its own beginning. Each chapter also was to be in some way—thematically, symbolically, parodically—a mirror image of the one before.

"Footnotes" meant to express the way I think we live, our days and actions little more than second thoughts, improvisations, elaborations, trills, upon some unperceived, unseen, probably imaginary text.

Going On, by contrast, was my fumbled attempt to insist upon an underlying unity, to imply connection among these disparate moments, to conjure up linearity.

That both story and novel were abandoned cannot mean nothing.

If we must learn to put our distress signals in code, perhaps it's not because that way lies communication, perhaps it's only because the codes seem so much more meaningful, so much more fraught, than are our lives. Because we have somehow to imagine ourselves larger than the sun's footprint. And if we can't have meaning, then at least we'll have the appearance of meaning: its promise, heft, import.

I'd first come across that phrase, You must learn to put your distress signals in code, while browsing through literary magazines at Beaucoup Books on Magazine. I bought the magazine and carried it off to Joe's (not Joe's from the Quarter but a later, uptown incarnation that soon folded), where, drinking my way into evening, I read the rest of the magazine yet managed to arrive home without it. Years later I'd been in the audience when the poet David Lunde came to UNO to read.

—Some of the things Deborah O'Neil and I talked about after her play on Sunday. A kind of heady conversation I seldom had. Guiltily looking about as we sat in Rue de la Course (also on Magazine) over coffee, tea and biscotti, feeling again like the undergraduate I'd been for only the shortest of times.

Deborah's play was the surprise she'd promised.

She told me about it over dinner at Commander's, fine paté, woody cabernet sauvignon, swordfish steak with béarnaise, grilled mushrooms, that amazing bread-pudding soufflé they do.

We slid into seats front row center moments before the show began. The theater was a warehouse off Julia Street whose conversion seemed as superficial and tenuous as any Hollywood set. Behind pressed-fiber walls there would be echoing spaces of bare support beams, girders thick with cobweb and grime, uninhabitable spaces. The whole thing could be struck in a few hours. Seats were of the stackable plastic sort—contoured, they call them, though for what species I can't imagine. People sat in suits and dresses, in torn jeans, flannel shirts, all black, in designer warm-ups and overalls and not much at all, sipping white jug wine from plastic cups.

Onstage, characters at a dinner party swirled in eccentric orbits about one another. Obviously few were familiars; conversation was mostly phatic, with sudden intrusions of intensely personal remarks that brought silence crashing down. Domestic employees ferried through with platters of drinks, squab, canapés, tureens, covered dishes, but would not be detained.

All the actors wore masks, and the very moment we thought we had one of them pegged (manipulative CEO, poor-little-me wife, kind-hearted friend) he or she would trade masks with one of the others and in so doing become a wholly different character.

Apparently there was also dissension among partygoers as to appropriate music. The sound track careened from Carl Orff to Willie Dixon to Sinatra to REM. At one point "Sympathy for the Devil" and the *1812* Overture played simultaneously.

Twenty minutes into the play (as I resisted impulses to pull out my notebook, start making lists, try to keep track of all this) one of the male actors left the stage and, stripping off everything but his mask, stepping into high heels and strapping on a tray like those cigarette vendors once wore, strode through the audience passing out still more masks. These were blank, but came with boxed crayons.

We were supposed to participate.

And some did, wonderfully.

The whole thing shimmered, changing again and again before our eyes—at once brilliant, prosaic, unheralded, obscene, chaotic, challenging, comforting, silly, obvious, disturbing.

A man in a three-piece gray suit and red smiley-face mask stood at the back of the hall and, claiming to be the play's author, confirming the disappointment he'd anticipated even from its inception, demanded that the production immediately be shut down.

Another, an emissary (he said) from the Arts Council in Washington, mask remaining blank, a form, praised free expression in America in drumlike manner.

One rose and, having brought a hush to the house with an imploring wave of his hand, wearing no mask at all, simply stood weeping.

Finally the cigarette vendor threw a kimono over substantial shoulders. Stepping back onstage, he said, "The rest is silence. Unless . . ."

He paused.

". . . I have a higher bid?"

And the curtain fell.

To resounding applause.

My own not the least, once I'd shaken myself loose from the spell. Even to move, I felt, somehow would violate what I'd just experienced, bring mundane life crashing back in.

"Too pretentious, isn't it?" Deborah said beside me. "I *knew* it. I don't know why I let them—"

When I told her it was among the most powerful moments of theater I'd seen, she shut up and sat staring at me. All around us people stood, easing back into ordinary lives.

"You're desperate, Lewis."

Of course. But that was hardly new.

Still in his kimono, heels exchanged for platform slippers, the cigarette vendor came out with a dozen red roses for Deborah. She ducked her face into them.

"How embarrassing."

But couldn't escape standing to acknowledge the applause when it didn't stop.

When she did stand, swaying, I thought again, as I'd thought when I first saw her, of willows.

Afterwards, then, we repaired to Rue de la Course, there over French roast, Earl Grey and biscotti to speak of grand ideas, ambition, disappointment, high rent and sleeping alone, ghosts, phantoms, demands of the past.

This part of town had just begun to crawl out from under years of abandon and disrepair as first young people, then investors, bought up the old Humpty-Dumpty houses and started putting them back together again. Even now, this late at night, a crew was at work across the street on a swayback Colonial double, portions of which had been painted dull silver, like aircraft models. Three men on ladders, spotlights directed up towards them as they scraped, sandpapered, sprayed, and hammered.

Deborah sat watching them. "You sure it wasn't too pretentious?"

No. Want another tea?

Why not.

I went inside. When I came out balancing full mugs, the workers across the street had stopped and begun packing everything—wire brushes, sanders, paint, ladders, toolboxes, toolbelts, lights—into trucks and hatchbacks.

"Thanks," Deborah said. She drank. "What part did you like best?"

"Intellectually?"

"Whatever."

"Okay. I have to tell you: I found the guy wandering around nude in the audience a real turn-on."

"Yeah. Me too. You ready to go, Lewis?"

O yes.

17

YEARS AGO A New Orleans friend named Chris Smither wrote a song called "Love You Like a Man," a fierce, intensely physical encomium detailing what his woman needs, what she's not going to find elsewhere and what *he* can do if she'd only give him the chance; these days, Chris says up in Boston where he lives now, he performs it chiefly as a nostalgia piece.

However we might laugh it off, over time our lives' landmark days become more commemorative than celebratory. Passing years find us able to care passionately about less and less. *Less* becomes what we're capable of as well, physically, emotionally—and finally what we hope for, what we believe still possible.

No: not the précis of another heady discussion with Deborah O'Neil, though it might have been. And though Deborah was directly responsible. For as I came to spend more and more time with her, within myself I sensed all manner of rumblings and unsettlings, felt systems I'd thought shut down for good start kicking over again.

Lights flare, dim, dim further still—and finally catch. The survivors let out a long breath.

The long-disused engine turns over once, again, stalls with power surging audibly towards it before stuttering into full bloom. The castaways will be able to escape after all.

It's alive! spectators cry out in horror films.

Holy words.

Somehow we go on being given new chances.

—What I was thinking Sunday night (or Monday morning, whichever shore you watched from), having left Deborah's a little after one. Lying with body exhausted, mind chugging away, in a bamboolike shaft of moonlight.

Late that afternoon I'd come home and, on my hurried way towards a shower and new clothes, gone into the kitchen for a bottle of water only to find refrigerator, pantry and shelves stocked for the first time in years. With no one to cook for, I'd long ago given it up. I ate out or nibbled at plates of cheese, crackers, sausage, raw vegetables.

A note scrawled in huge printed letters across three sheets of 8 ½ X 11 paper, taped to the refrigerator door like a child's school drawings put up on display, read:

I FRIED YOUR LAST EGG FOR BREAKFAST. IT WAS RIPE.

THEN AS YOU MAY HAVE NOTICED I WENT SHOPPING. SOMEONE HAS TO. FIGURE SINCE I DON'T HAVE A JOB I'LL TAKE UP A HOBBY AT LEAST AND GET DOWN TO SOME GOURMET COOKING. ALWAYS MEANT TO.

NOTICED HOW THE GUTTERS ARE ALL CHOCKFULL BY THE WAY. THEY AND MOST OF THE SHUTTERS DONE PULLED WAY FROM THE WALL. FIGURE I CAN FIX THAT THE NEXT DAY OR TWO IF IT'S OKAY WITH YOU.

THERE'S SOME OTHER STUFF TOO. WE CAN TALK ABOUT IT. PROBABLY NEVER TOLD YOU, BUT MY OLD MAN WAS A CARPENTER, HANDYMAN, UP ROUND TUPELO. I WAS ALWAYS KIND OF ASHAMED OF HIM WHEN I WAS A KID.

I'LL BE OUT LOOKING FOR WORK WHILE YOU'RE OUT WORKING. LET ME KNOW WHEN YOU'LL BE HOME AND THERE'LL BE A HOT MEAL WAITING.

THANKS, ZEKE

P.S. I STARTED THE NOVEL THIS AFTERNOON, I'D JUST WATCHED ZEBRAHEAD ON TV. AMAZING, ALL THIS CABLE CHANNEL STUFF. CALLING THE GUY IN MY BOOK LEW GRIFFIN FOR NOW. THAT OKAY?

Of the six messages on my answering machine, the most important was from Tulane, basically *Hello? hello? is anyone there?* Like a message launched blindly into space.

I would have called back right then, but nobody'd be around on

Sunday afternoon. I'd missed, what, one class? It seemed like more. This week had been all over the damn place. Felt as though I needed a map and one of those time-lines-of-history charts.

"So many things happen to us," Deborah said, arm passing into light from the window as she gathered the pink cotton blanket loosely about her. She sat, knees drawn up, against the headboard. "How are we ever supposed to know which are the important ones, which ones matter?"

"We're not. Maybe the ones that matter are the ones we *decide* matter."

"I'd love to believe we have that much control over it." She sipped white wine from a tulip-shaped glass. "You never drink, do you?"

"Only because for a long time that was mostly what I did. A lot of those things you say you don't know about, things that are important and matter, things that don't, got lost forever because of it. Like people sinking into quicksand in old movies. You watch them go down. In your own disabled way you try to hold on to them. Then you're there at the edge of the frame alone again."

"My father was a drinker."

I made no reply. Became a receptacle.

"He'd been a tyrant a long time, I guess. Told my mother what to fix for dinner every night, how much she could spend on the household that week, when she could buy shoes for herself or the older kids. And he'd fly into these smashing, screaming fits of rage when things went wrong. But by the time I came along—I was a late child, a surprise, my mother turned forty the year after—he'd become an invalid, someone my mother had to care for totally. Wet brain, she called it. Mostly what I remember is the first time I brought a friend home from school. Had to be nine, ten years old, I guess. Mom would prop him up in a chair in front of the TV. She'd tie a sheet around him to keep him from getting up and wandering off, and she made these diapers out of old towels.

"So Sue Ann Goerner and I came in after school—my oldest sister, who stayed with him most days, had just left, Mom was due home from work at the diner up the street within the hour—and he's sitting there a few steps inside the front door. One of those classic shotguns: you look straight through the house, four or five rooms, and see banana trees in the backyard. Remember stereopticons? *Hazel* was on TV. He'd pawed at the diaper till he'd got it pushed down enough that he was able to reach in and get his penis. When Sue Ann and I walk in, he's sitting there playing with it, pumping away at this thing for all he's worth with his eyes never leaving Shirley Booth, though God knows nothing was ever going to come of it.

"What's he doing? Sue Ann asked, and I told her, finessing details I wasn't a hundred percent sure about now that I'd unexpectedly become the voice of authority. Went on for some time. You have anything to eat? she said when I was through.

"I remember thinking how my father's thing looked like one of the slugs that came out at night and ate leftover cat food out back."

She finished her wine and set the glass on the floor.

"That became pretty much his life, such as it was. Sitting propped up in front of *Dallas*, *I Dream of Jeannie*, or *The Rockford Files* in improvised diapers, trying to whack off. He died when I was twelve. It's mostly the tenderness I remember, this incredible tenderness my mother showed for this man who'd so terribly abused her."

I moved up beside her and she leaned into me.

"I could end that way too, Lew." I felt the heat of her tears on my skin.

"We all can. All too easily."

Her finger traced the crater of a gunshot wound on my shoulder, a knife scar low in my ribs. The first looked like a smallpox vaccination, the second like a zipper, or the backbone of some tiny animal.

"You're one of the important things, Lew. This matters."

I didn't respond, just pulled her closer to me.

"Okay. So it's romantic abandon you want, huh?"

"You have some?"

"Sure. Hang on, let me open a can. To tell the truth, there's a surplus. Lots of supply, no demand. How's your slug, by the way?"

My slug was fine.

And now both slug and I had crawled home. One of us, at least, to sleep.

All day Sunday, I'd been out there beating bushes.

Hauled myself out of bed at seven, sliding from under Bat, asleep on my chest, to face a workingman's breakfast of scrambled eggs, grits with jalapeños and cheese, toast, melon. Might as well use all this food, since it was here. Bat felt the same way, circling back to his bowl again and again, mewing shrilly, as I ate. Drank a pot of coffee with breakfast and another afterwards while cleaning up the kitchen.

Nerves honed to a fine point.

Whereupon I hit the streets.

There are several groups of people who make it their business to know who's in town, to notice new arrivals, take note of weaknesses and dependencies. Some are (as they like to say) "with the government." Some work for even older and still more centralized, if far-flung, organizations. A few are independents.

None more independent than Doo-Wop.

Actually, it's difficult to think of Doo-Wop ever being sufficiently integrated into the common society as even to be considered independent of, apart, or exempt from it.

John Donne, obviously, never went drinking with him.

On the other hand, there weren't a lot of others who hadn't. And if so, he knew their stories. Had them fixed forever, flies in amber, in his memory.

That time of day, it was relatively easy to find him. He'd be near one end or the other of his regular route. Some days he started uptown and worked his way into the Quarter, others he did it in reverse. I took a guess. It was a little before nine when I got to Lafitte's and the bartender, pushing a mop around the floor, avoiding things like tables and chair legs and walls as though magnetically repelled, told me I'd just missed Doo-Wop. The bartender wore a stained, unironed white poet's shirt so oversize that it resembled a dress. He was completely bald on top, hair at the side of his head long and twisted into little pigtails. Looked like Pippi Longstocking after a sex change.

"He did boost one drink from the guy that was here. A beer, if you can believe it. Just sat there looking at it, shaking his head. Pure crow's pickings around here 'less it's a weekend or there's a convention or some kind of a ball game in town. Guy comes in here this early, he's gonna be lucky to have enough to buy his *own* drink. And he ain't likely to care much of a hoot 'bout other people's stories or his own, know what I mean?"

That's what Doo-Wop did: roamed the city, trading stories for drinks. Like Homer, the Middle Ages' wandering minstrels, Celtic harpists such as O'Carolan, China's ancient poets.

So I went up the steps one by one.

Kenny's Shamrock on Burgundy, about the size of cinder-block toilets you find in parks or roadside stops and smelling not unlike them, Ireland travel posters stapled to the walls.

Donna's on Rampart across from Louis Armstrong Park, good burgers and bar food, great brass-band music nights and weekends.

A bar on St. Ursulines that to the best of my knowledge has never had a name. Same bartender and to all appearances the same patrons have been there for twenty years. I guess they all go home sometime, but it doesn't seem like it.

I caught up with him at Monster's. It had started life as a disco about the time discos were dying out, then briefly managed to transform itself into a concert hall for the likes of Don McLean, Arlo Guthrie, John Lee Hooker. Mirror balls still hung over a dance floor crowded with stacked plastic chairs and unlit. Posters curled and cracked on the walls beside signed photographs of musicians no one had ever heard of, some of them in leisure suits, tie-dye, Nehru jackets, Carnaby gear.

"My man," Doo-Wop said to my reflection in the mirror behind the bar. Silver had worn away in patches, erasing portions of the world. "Been a while."

We'd known each other now for over thirty years. This was his standard greeting. Sometimes I'd be *My man*, other times *Captain*. Names weren't a big thing with Doo-Wop. *Been a while* was equally generic, since Doo-Wop had no conception of time. For him everything happened in the present. Hopi Mean Time, a friend once called it.

"Buy you a drink?"

Part of the ritual. New Orleans is a Catholic city, a pagan, voodoo city. It takes ritual to its heart.

Doo-Wop paused, head tilting first right, then left, as though sampling winds. "Bourbon," he decided.

But Monster's has been hanging by its fingernails for too many years. Employees figure if they're gonna go down with it, why break a sweat. Makes it hard to motivate them. Glaring across the bar didn't work. Dropping a ten onto it did.

Bourbon appeared before Doo-Wop. He poured it straight down. In its former life the shot glass had been someone's souvenir of Florida.

"Something I do keep wondering," Doo-Wop said.

I signaled for another bourbon. Wondering how long my luck and my ten will hold out.

"None of my business, of course." He sniffed this new shot of generic whiskey as though it's been aged in barrels. "You ever find any of these folks you show up asking me about?"

"Some of them, sure."

"They want to get found?"

"Some of them."

He nodded and threw the bourbon back. Waited quietly. I glanced at the bartender. He put down another, but his look let me know I was pushing it.

Doo-Wop's look, on the other hand, let me know we were ready for business.

"Name's Armantine Rauch," I told him. "Twentyish, black, knows his way around. May be freelancing as enforcement for street bankers. Scamming, definitely—and it could be almost anything. Started off his career stealing money from a relative's purse, soon went on to bigger and better things. Boosted cars, stabbed one of his teachers in the chest with a pair of scissors."

"Boy's busy."

I nodded.

"From around here?"

"He is now. State's been taking care of him the last few years. Sprung him this past August."

"Taking care of himself again."

I showed him my copy of a photo Don had pulled up from prison files. These shots are shaky at best. Add the fax machine's contribution, it could be anyone from Pancho Villa to Charley Patton.

"Nice photo."

Right.

And for Doo-Wop, downright garrulous.

"Don't look much like him, though."

Ah.

I dropped another ten on the bar just as the air conditioner heaved itself to life, catching up the bill in its sudden draft. The bartender snagged it neatly with one hand as he set down Doo-Wop's shot with the other.

Doo-Wop sat considering.

"Tommy T's Tavern, out on Gentilly."

I knew the place. Any given time, half the guys in there were cons, the other half ex-military. Cons, I could handle. I understood them. Only fools felt safe around the others. You never knew what might set them off, which way they'd go with it, how far or hard.

"Owe you one, Captain." Doo-Wop had a finely developed sense of just compensation. To his mind the drinks I'd bought him exceeded the value of the information he was able to give me, so next time was on him. And he damned sure wouldn't forget.

"One other thing," he said as I stood to leave.

"Okay."

"Take Papa with you? He don't get out near enough. Probably be up at Kinney's about now, you stop by there."

"Doesn't get out, huh."

"Kinney's? Far as Papa's concerned, that's the same as staying home."

18

WITHIN THE HOUR Papa and I were out there, sitting in a back corner at a table with four legs of unequal length and warped floorboards beneath—it's like a lock or puzzle, you keep turning the table, hoping to hit the right combination, feel things fall into place—with mugs of barely chilled, watery beer. The mugs made quiet sucking sounds when we lifted them off the table. Forearms clung to tabletops sticky for twenty years despite daily scouring. The dominant smells were Lysol and old grease. The dominant fashions were muscle shirts, T-shirts and tattoos.

My coat and tie, and my black face, stood out like a cardinal in a flock of penguins.

No one in there could keep his eyes away from our table. They huddled together in groups, talking among themselves, glancing again and again in our direction. Till one of them, finally, couldn't keep nose, balls, ego and White Pride in check any longer.

Stepping so close that his legs touched the table, he looked straight on at Papa. I'm not sitting there. The sleeves of his black T are rolled.

"Welcome to Tommy T's," he told Papa. "Don't remember seeing you in here before."

Papa sighed. "You *haven't* seen me in here before."

"Well then, don't be a stranger from now on. I'm Wayne."

He glanced around at the others to see how he was doing. Just so there'd be no distractions, someone pulled the plug on the jukebox. Three notes up the four-note climb into dominant and chorus, Hank

Williams Jr. stopped singing. What was coming up was sure to be better entertainment.

"But you gotta know to leave your boy there outside, right? His kind ain't never been welcome here. Won't *ever* be."

Papa looked up at him. Papa was stamped from the same pattern as a lot of them in there, brush-cut hair, leathery face. But he'd been fighting undisclosed wars, leading other men into those wars and losing a lot of them, good men and bad wars, bad wars and good men, when Wayne was grunting his first diapers full of disposable goods.

"Boy," Papa said after a moment. The word hung in the air between them. It's just been slapped up on a fence, paint's still dripping from it. I saw Papa's muscles relax, his breathing slow—though he was thinking about none of this.

He put his hands flat on the table.

"Now boy, I know you can't much help being the stupid asshole son of a bitch you are. It's what your folks were before you, God bless 'em. How you gonna be anything else? I understand that. We all do."

He looked around the room.

"So I'm not gonna take offense at anything you just said. Considering the source and all. Instead, I'm gonna offer to buy everyone in here a round. What the hell, a couple of rounds."

There was a pause as all the mathematicians worked on this new equation in a formula they thought sure they already knew.

Seems to me they're drawing closer to our table. As up closer to the blackboard, scowling at figures there? This is probably paranoia, I think. No it's not, I think.

Muscles bunched and tattoos on biceps puckered as Wayne reached across the table for Papa's neck.

Sometimes I almost forget how naked and ugly their hatred can be. But I saw it then in his eyes. Old man and a nigger. Teach this white man a lesson, fuck that nigger up bad, then get back to his drinks and friends. Simple plan. Way things were meant to be.

Wayne's arm was halfway across the table when his face moved suddenly away from us, back and down—like the detective's on those stairs in *Psycho*. His head hit the floor. Papa's hooked a foot behind his ankle and pulled him over.

Then Papa was down there too, with his knee planted in Wayne's genitals and a thumb on his carotid.

Suddenly light flooded the bar. A voice from the open doorway said: "You through playing with him, Captain, you let that young idiot up off the floor. Assuming he's able to get up. He can't, we'll just dump him out back. Not like anyone gives half a shit, is it."

The door swung shut behind him, closing us back into darkness.

"Gene, plug that jukebox in. Rest of you either get the fuck about your business or out of here."

The clientele swarmed back to drinks, TV shows, pool tables, conversations. Hank Williams Jr. abrupted into the IV chord. Free at last.

The man dragged a chair over from the next table and sat down with us. He and Papa grinned at one another. I wondered where he left the wheelbarrows he usually carried around on his shoulders.

"Jack," Papa said. "So you own bars now instead of tearing them up."

"Mostly."

"Heard you were still in Cambodia."

"I was."

"Sue Ling doing okay, I hope."

"Believe it."

Papa nodded. "Always thought that girl had fine taste. Then she up and married you."

"Hear *you* moved up in the world too, Captain. But they call you Papa now, don't they? Make your money off what *other* people do."

Papa shrugged.

"Hey," the man said. "Maybe you already did enough, all those years, who's to say. Buy you a beer?"

"Sure."

These came from under the bar, in bottles. Beads of cold sweat on them.

The man sat looking down at Wayne. "You think that boy's gonna get up?"

"He'll come around. He's strong."

"Good thing, too, dumb as he is."

They grinned at one another again for a while.

"Don't guess you showed up here just for old times' sake," the man said.

Papa shook his head, then looked at me.

"Lew Griffin," I said, putting my hand across the table. He didn't take it.

I told him about Armantine Rauch, and why I was looking for him. Described his appearance and background. Slid the photo across the table, which tried to keep it. Told him we'd greatly appreciate any help he could give us.

When I was done, he looked at Papa. "What's this all about, Bill?" I'd never heard anyone call Papa by name before.

"Talk to him, not me," Papa said. He sipped at his beer. "I just run the ferry."

"Right." Throwing back half his Dos Equis. "Okay, I guess I owe you that, at least." The second half of his beer went looking for the first.

"Griffin. That right? Man you're looking for, this Rauch, yeah, he comes in here some."

"How often?"

"Some, I said."

"Once a week? Paydays? Every night?"

"Look. Till ATF says I have to, I don't keep track."

"You know where he lives?"

"Around, is what I heard."

"You consider having your people give me a call next time he shows up?"

He glanced over at Papa, who nodded.

"Okay."

"Thanks. We—"

"But you want to look him up before then, he teaches a self-defense class over at the high school every Sunday."

I asked for directions and got them.

"That it?"

I nodded.

"Appreciate it, Jack," Papa replied. "You be sure to give Sue Ling my love."

When he was gone, we sat looking down at Wayne.

"Good work, by the way," I told Papa. "Guess Doo-Wop figured I might need you out here. Usually have to do my own heavy lifting."

Papa drained off the last of his beer.

"Yeah. Well, good thing once in a while to just kick back, let somebody else do the cooking."

When I got home that afternoon three police cars were parked a couple of blocks up my street. Cops stood talking to people and writing on clipboards as radios sputtered. The kids on bikes had grabbed another purse and a wallet from an old couple out for a walk. One of my neighbors had chased them halfway to Freret.

19

YOU COULD READ the building's transformations through the years, manifest history, in its string of add-ons and embellishments: the colonnaded entryway that turned it from palatial residence to luxury hotel sometime in the fifties; redundant entrances from subsequent incarnation as apartment building with (judging from electric meters left in place on the rear wall) at least twelve units; from its brief time as church, a long-unused plywood marquee, FIRST UNITY emerging, ghostlike, beneath whitewash.

Now it was a school. Fleurs-de-lis and stylized coat-of-arms medallions high on the walls had been highlighted in peach, as had miniature, rooklike turrets at the roofline. The remainder of the building was light blue. Behind the building, riverside, half a dozen aluminum trailers squatted on high cinder-block foundations with stairways out front, intended to be temporary, auxiliary classrooms, now permanent.

The school on this late Saturday afternoon looked abandoned.

The front fence, facing on Joseph, was impassable, looped in lengths of chain and padlocked. Around to the side near the back, though, was an old delivery entrance. Roots from a nearby oak had shattered its drive to plugs of cement sitting all on different planes, vaguely geodesic, with shoots of grass and weed between them. The gate stood agap. There was a long groove in the cement where the gate had been forced open until it would go no farther, forward or back, and had remained so ever since.

I was crabbing through this gap, thinking I'd come too late, no one's here, it's a waste of time, when a young woman appeared outside a utility shed lodged at the lot's far corner. After a moment others began to emerge, individually, in pairs or small groups. Most wore gym clothes. Fleece shorts, sleeveless T's and sweats, warm-ups. A few in skintight biker's shorts or cutoff jeans.

I watched as they slipped through the fence on their way back to cars, cups of coffee, Blockbuster videos, showers, drinks, apartments, homes. Stragglers included an elaborately coiffed fiftyish woman in silver warm-ups, a pair of black-clad silent teenagers, an elderly male so bent with arthritis that his face was parallel to the ground.

Was that it?

I waited.

Faint strands of music from inside. Something with a ¾ beat, heavy bass.

The music shut off, and moments later a man stepped out. He wore an unreconstructed silk sportcoat over maroon T-shirt and chinos, carried a backpack and portable CD player. Pulling the door shut behind him, he glanced my way, but his eyes passed on. Then he seemed to remember something he'd forgotten or left behind, and went back into the building.

Towards which I was moving, fast.

I went through the front door just in time to see, out a back window, the chain-link fence rebounding where he'd gone over. It still sang against its posts. The window was never intended for exits, sudden or otherwise. Its frame hung by a corner, tapping alternately at fence and building side, snap-in plastic shutters dropping one by one to the ground.

A quick movement off in trees, worthy of Bigfoot or Deerslayer.

You live the way Rauch does, you *better* have good instincts and reflexes.

Somehow he'd sensed I was there. *Knew* I was there.

I went back inside. The floor, which also served as foundation, was cheap cement, poured quickly, pitted and uneven. Exercise mats were scattered about, folding steel chairs pushed together helter-skelter at the back. Two or three were capsized. Rauch had gone up over them to get to the window.

I'd reconnoitered before coming in, of course. The trees, half a block of them, were there to close the school off (symbolically, but it's a city of symbols) from streets behind. Those treeless streets bore derelict rows of single-family residences divided and redivided into housing for double, triple that or more. Front porches sinking like elephants onto their knees, forsaken appliances, crippled furniture and tireless cars forever at curbside. Sun's fingers peeling paint off the sides of houses. Bodies of rats and squirrels bloating on sidewalks, beneath houses, in the mouths of sewer drains.

The city's tradition of corner grocers lived on here, though, and through the trees, connecting school and spurned neighborhood, where at Mr. Lee's store burgers, tacos, nachos and fries could be purchased, electronic games be played, years of students had worn and maintained a path.

I went over the fence and along that path and emerged just moments after Rauch.

As he came out of the trees, a black Honda Civic swung around the corner from Joseph and pulled in at the curb before him. Rauch peered into it—to all appearances as surprised as I was to see Shon Delany there in the car—and got in.

I was half a block off when the Honda pulled away. In the rearview mirror Shon watched me sprint towards them, slow and stop. I jotted down the license number in my notebook. These days, I trusted very little to memory.

I went back through the trees to the outbuilding, where I failed to find the clues any good detective surely would have, then took a bus home, where, before leaving again for dinner with Deborah and (as it turned out) her play, I sat at the kitchen table looking up at Zeke's note on the refrigerator door and thinking about prison.

Over the years I've spent scattered weekends and overnights in jail, three or four longer layouts as convenient suspect, detainee by caprice, material witness. But there's also one extended stretch—not on record, but floating around if you know where to look, who to ask, in some Platonic shadowland between the ideal and real.

What happened was, I got picked up on Dryades, half a block down from my rented room, for matching the description of someone who had held up a store on Jackson and shot its owner when he pulled a lead pipe with tape on one end out from under the counter.

Matching the description was a joke, of course. Cops (those days white, the only kind) were on the lookout for a young black man. Big and dangerous looking, reports said. That was, what? 65 percent of anyone out on the street in that part of town? Eye of the beholder. But there I was, fortunate enough to be stumbling along as the prowl car drove by. And since I was drunk—this may have been one of my earliest blackouts—not only couldn't I answer questions to their satisfaction, I was so befuddled I didn't even know what was going on.

One moment I'd been doggedly slogging my way towards home, the next I was facedown on the sidewalk with arms behind me and an officer's knee in my kidney. Some of it came back to me later in bits and pieces, fragments, like a series of unrelated snapshots.

When I woke up hours later on a steel bench, two guys were leaning over me. Hard to believe human breath could smell that bad. One had eyes set at the sides of his face like a fish's and a nose that looked like a new potato. The other's eyes were set so close only his hatchetlike nose kept them apart. These guys had about six teeth between them.

"Nigguh comin' roun', Bo."

Answered by a grunt.

The first speaker was the one whose bladderlike hand covered my throat. The grunt came from farther off. I tried to flex my legs and couldn't. He was holding them down.

"Been a while since we had us dark meat."

Something between giggle and gag by way of response, footwards, from the other.

I reached up suddenly, without opening my eyes, and snapped the first one's thumb. As he reflexively pulled away, I seized his forearm and hand, and broke the wrist between them.

Then I did the fastest sit-up of my life—easier with him holding down my legs like a good coach—and snagged number two's hair in my hand. His head bent back, his arms loosened on my legs. I took him down to the floor, falling on top. Drove my fist into his throat. He tried at the same time to scream and draw a breath, and couldn't do either.

Everything in the cell had stopped, gone on hold, for the eight seconds this took. Now people started moving again, conversations started back up.

Nobody saw anything, of course, when the Man asked. What fight? Hey, they'd all been asleep.

I spent almost two weeks, shuttled from cell to cell, in the cement belly of that beast, habeas corpus nowhere on the horizon.

It was Frankie DeNoux who found out where I was and sent his lawyer to pry me loose. Frankie was a bail bondsman I sometimes worked for, and I spent a few weeks then working for his lawyer, writing letters, tending files and running errands, until I'd paid off what I owed him. My place on Dryades had been rented out to someone else while I was gone, so Frankie's lawyer let me sleep in the supply room.

It was a long time after that before I pulled things back together. You live as close to the ground as I did then, it doesn't take much to put you the rest of the way down. And if you have good sense, as in any fight, once you're down you stay there.

Years later, with far more light behind my life though for the moment not much anywhere else, since power had gone off all over the city hours ago, I woke—I'd been on a case, without sleep, for three days—and turned onto my back to find myself staring up at dark, rolling sky. A hurricane had swept through as I slept, slicing away the roof. At that very moment lightning flashed, all but blinding me, and power came back on. The air conditioner wheezed a single long breath and kicked in. The Vivaldi bassoon concerto to which I'd been listening hours ago, before the outage, resumed.

Though they occurred years apart and with no apparent connection, these two incidents, when I look back, always fall together in my mind.

I sat there looking up at Zeke's note on the refrigerator, thinking how our lives weave, dodge, collide.

The first thing I noticed when I got sober, really sober (after, what, thirty years or more?) was how *ordinary* everything was.

I remembered Alouette in her farewell note: *I tried so hard, I really did. I hope you can give me credit for that. But everything's so ordinary now, so plain.*

I remembered Marlowe's speech to bounceback drunk Terry Lennox in *The Long Goodbye*: "It's a different world. You have to get used to a paler set of colors, a quieter lot of sounds."

And I remembered Hosie Straughter.

"Our lives can be taken away from us at any time, Lew. Suspended, assumed by others, devalued, destroyed. Snap a finger and they're gone."

We were in a bar on Decatur. Days before, Hosie's lover Esmé had been shot by Carl Joseph, the sniper I'd later watch go off a roof as I pursued him.

For a long time then we were both quiet. Hosie raised his glass and drank, raised it again to peer through it at the light, much as Esmé had done. Traffic sounds came from the street outside. Through the bar's propped-open door we watched morning begin.

"Don't ever forget that, Lewis."

A drunken college student staggered by, bounced off the front wall, rebounded into the street and went on.

"You want another one?"

I shrugged.

"Sure you do. Only help you'll ever get. A few hard drinks and morning."

Our glasses were refilled. Hosie raised his to me.

> "Good-bye, good luck, struck the sun and the moon,
> To the fisherman lost on the land.
> He stands alone at the door of his home,
> With his long-legged heart in his hand."

Then: "Dylan Thomas. And the best we can hope for."

Maybe it is. Home is the sailor home from the sea and the hunter home from the hill. Bringing back, for all his terrible efforts, all his expense of spirit, only what remains now of himself.

So many holes in my life. Small ones, day-sized, weeklong, owing to drink and disavowal; others, deeper and farther reaching, to various inabilities and inactions. An entire year gone to blood loss, hospitals, drugs, and afternoon TV when I was shot that second time. When La-Verne leaned above me saying (possibly I only imagined this), "You want the hole to take over, don't you, Lew? It's not enough any more just to stand close and peer over the edge. You want the hole to come after you."

It did, of course.

True, there were times it seemed I hardly cared what happened to me. At some level, I suppose, I half hoped for the worst—became a kind of magnet for it. Walked into situations no rational man would breach. Set myself up for disaster again and again like some dime-store windup doomsday machine.

But I never lost sight of how perilous every moment of our life is, how frail and friable the tissue holding self and world together.

Only the luckiest ever get to show up at the door with long-legged heart in hand.

Hosie lowered his glass.

"Don't ever forget her, either. Esmé, I mean. We have to pass it on, Lewis, what we've loved, what's mattered to us. If we don't—"

His hand turned palm up, as though to hold for a moment the world's emptiness.

"I'm so tired of talking, Lew. Tired of the sound of my own voice."

I put my hand in his, there on the bar.

20

SOMETIMES, HOSIE, DESPITE your advice, despite my own understanding that this, memory, is the sole enduring life I have, I wish I *could* forget.

At some level, of course, forgetting is what the drinking was all about, along with other holes in my life. And forgetting (I know now) is the sea into which my son David set sail.

Looking back at what I've written thus far, these many twists and turns of chronology, I wonder if, in some strange way, forgetting may not be what I've been about here as well. Putting things down to discharge them. Working to tuck memories safely away in the folds and trouser cuffs of time.

Moments ago I pulled out a legal pad and, reading back through these two hundred–some pages, tried to plot out, tried to untangle and write down sequentially, the sequence of events.

Let's see: I'd already been stomped by those kids out on Derbigny when Zeke showed up, right? And dinner with Deborah, attending her play, was that before or after Papa and I encountered the great white hopes (definitely lowercase) out Gentilly way? Just where does my first meeting Deborah fit into all this? Or finding the body in that tract house on Old Metairie Road?

All a kind of temporal plaid.

Memory's always more poet than reporter.

Proust at the barricades.

Or Faulkner struggling with the screenplay for *The Big Sleep*. He can't figure out what order all this is supposed to have happened in and in desperation finally calls up Chandler himself. When I wrote that, Chandler tells him, only God and I knew what I meant—and now I've forgotten.

Maybe I don't have that right. Maybe that's not Faulkner and Chandler at all, but the director calling up Faulkner once the script's been done: how the hell am I supposed to shoot this? Or for that matter someone, an editor, a reader, one of Faulkner's hunting buddies, trying to figure out *The Sound and the Fury*.

Memory's never been much of a timekeeper. Always whispers, "Trust me." Never one, though, to show up when needed, keep its room clean, do laundry, bathe on a regular basis.

But *lord* (as granddaddy Chappelle might have said if he'd ever thought much about such things, sitting on his back porch outside Forrest City with a jelly glass of bourbon, plug of tobacco, and the knothole he spit through, with swarms of lightning bugs and three generations of children swooping around, himself quite a storyteller), *lord* what stories it tells.

21

MONDAY MORNING WENT by, as I once read in some mystery or another, in a blaze of inaction. See Lew haul himself from bed around noon, after getting home from Deborah's a little before 2 A.M. See Lew make coffee. See Lew fall asleep over the *Times-Picayune*. See Lew go back to bed. See Bat walk on Lew's head because he hasn't been fed. See Bat give up and go away.

Monday morning the license number I'd scribbled down as the black Honda pulled away got me nowhere.

It did get me a free lunch.

"Stolen," Don had said on the phone. He'd been away from it maybe three minutes. "From a parking lot out on Airline. Tell me you're surprised."

"Not really."

"Okay, then tell me why anyone would boost a Honda, for godsake. A *Honda*?" To someone at his end: "I'm on the phone here, Jack, you see that? That alright with you, my taking a phone call? Huh?" Then to me: "Any interest in taking me away from all this?"

"Not that hard up, old friend."

"Sure you are. Look, Lew, I gotta get out of here, talk to someone, look at someone, who's not a cop. Right now I'd just as soon shoot the lot of them. What the hell, it's almost eleven. Buy you lunch."

"Where you plan on taking me?"

"Picky date, huh."

"You want quality time, you pay for it."

"I guess Lucky Dogs are out?"

Silence in the wires.

"Manuel's Tamales, then. Cart's usually down on the corner by now."

I may have humphed, or whistled a bar or two of Bobby McFerrin's "Don't Worry, Be Happy."

"Okay, okay. Praline Connection do the trick?"

"Frenchmen, right?" There were two, one in the Faubourg Marigny, close to the river, another uptown, in the warehouse district. Same food, but they might as well be in separate countries.

"You got it. Thirty minutes?"

"Sure." You can be any place in New Orleans in thirty minutes.

Sitting already over his second beer as I came in, Don pushed an envelope across the table to me. Documents inside tracked the black Honda, a rental car up till thirteen months ago and sixty thousand miles, then sold at auction. Mostly rented instate. Computer-generated list of clients, stat of the title showing sale to one George Van Zandt, current registration, police theft report. It had been taken off a lot outside an abandoned bowling alley and across from a tiny Chinese restaurant much favored by the Metairie lunchtime crowd.

"Hope it helps," Don said.

Then Philip, one of the owners, looking the very image of the restaurant's cameolike logo in white shirt, tie, hat and close-cropped beard, was there to take our order. Fried chicken and another beer for Don, lima beans, rice and iced tea for me.

A parade of thirty or more young people went by in the street outside, curiously silent for all their number and collective motion, as though the wraparound windows were soundproof or the whole thing on TV with the volume off. The effect was eerie, unsettling, like peering into another world. Half a block behind the others, two young men held aloft a banner: HOW LONG CAN WE REMAIN SILENT?

"You were saying," I told Don, "how you were about to go postal."

He shook his head, drank before he spoke.

"Sometimes I look around me in the squad room and I think: I'm all alone here, the rest aren't human, any of them. But if they're not human, what are they?

"It wears you down, I know that, what you see day after day, how little you can do about any of it. You just keep slapping on patches, trying to hold yourself together. Trying to protect yourself, too, I guess. Finally you have so many patches there's not much left of the coat."

As so often, we think we're speaking of others and actually speak of ourselves. A point not lost on Don.

"There's one part of me that more than anything wants civility back, Lew. People saying please and thank you, opening doors for one another, letting other cars go first, keeping quietly and politely to themselves. I don't know. Maybe that's some kind of Republican dream, looking back at something that was really never there, trying to re-create it."

Philip brought our food, along with a fistful of hot sauces in bottles. I sprinkled clear Crystal over my beans and rice.

"Another part just wants it all *stopped*, the crime, the killing—and that part doesn't really care much how. That part scares me. To hell, it says, with civility. To hell with individual rights, due process, equal protection under the law. Constitution? Democracy? Civil rights? Nice ideas, folks, really fine. You hold on to those, you hear? But right now let's put them up on the shelf where they belong and get on with real life, let's just get the goddamn job done."

I thought again how, because of poverty, polarity and crime, we've become a nation without real cities—one, instead, of fenced villages shoved up against one another—and how, because we have no cities, because increasingly we're afraid to venture out and engage the world and have in our playpens toys like TVs and on-line computers that we believe connect us but instead render us ever more apart, ever more distracted and discrete, we've become a nation without culture.

I suspect, of course, in my liberal heart of hearts, that it's all intimately connected. That losing sense of community and culture irrevocably erodes the soul.

We'd tramped this ground many times before, Don and I. I'd told him how in my late teens it came to me with the force of revelation that America's racial problem has never been so much racial as fundamentally (in this supposedly classless society) a class problem.

So there we were, two old farts singing their sad praise of yesterdays. One of them, who carried a gun, wanting people to be nice to one another again while authorities mowed down wrongdoers, the other, who'd learned better than to carry one, smiling out of a black face suspended forever between the anxieties and ambitions of two worlds.

I'd just read Madison Smartt Bell's novel about the Haitian slave uprising of 1795 (Toussaint-Louverture, remember? another early hero of mine) and paraphrased for Don what Bell had told a *Washington Post* interviewer. That now we're having our own race war, that it's a slow-motion race war, disguised as crime in the streets. And that nobody, black or white, wants to admit what's happening.

Which made me think, when I read it, of Chester Himes's apocalyptic late stories and novels.

Don nodded. Then his face lifted, following something outside, beyond the glass. My own eyes went around as the door opened. Don rose, chair legs rasping back loudly on the cement floor.

"Hey. Dad." Words evenly spaced, as though set up on blocks.

"Danny! You okay?"

"What? Hey, sure. What else'd I be? This's my friend Billy." Short bursts of sound.

"Bobby," his friend said, tall and thin and sharp-edged as a shaft of Johnson grass. He wore a black silk suit over a T-shirt with tails out. The T-shirt started off white, but that had been some time back.

"I wish you'd let me know when you're going to be away, Danny. I thought we had an agreement. Just pick up the phone. You know?"

"Hey, I meant to, I really did. Been real busy, though."

"Busy."

"Yeah. Got a new job. Good one this time."

Don looked at him, at his friend, then at me.

"Hellish long hours. Most nights I'm so beat it's all I can do to open up a can of chili and fall in bed."

Bobby said something that sounded like *Burr goman.*

Don said, "At least you have a place to sleep, then."

"What? Oh, sure. Sure I do. No problem. And money in my pocket. You bet. Just like I said it would be."

Bobby said something else to him, even lower, that I didn't catch.

"Look, Dad. I gotta go, okay? I'll call. Promise."

"Yeah. Yeah, sure you will. Take care, son."

We watched them go out and turn the corner back up towards the Quarter.

Don drank from his Abita. I sipped at my tea.

"He's not going to call," I said.

Don put his empty bottle down. "Not a chance in hell."

"You didn't ask where he was staying."

"He wouldn't have told me."

Don picked up a piece of chicken and put it back down, wiped grease from his fingers.

"It's a lot worse than you know, Lew."

"Things generally are."

"I love him, Lew. I really love him. And there's not one damn thing I can do to help him, or stop him. All I can do is stand by and watch it happen."

He looked down at his fried chicken the way a *houngan* might peer into spilled fresh entrails.

Signs and signals everywhere, if you just knew how to read them.

22

THEY WERE ACTUALLY still there waiting, most of them anyway, when I took the corner fast and walked in, totally unprepared. No notes, no books, just sweaty clothes and a worried smile on my face.

Felt just like my undergrad days at USNO, in fact.

It had suddenly come to me, on the streetcar back uptown, that this was Monday, and that Monday was a class day. I'd already missed all Wednesday's classes and half of today's. I asked the woman beside me, an older black woman sitting with knees far apart, stockings rolled to her ankles, what time it was.

One-forty. I could just about make it.

I just about did.

Two-ten on the classroom clock when I got there. Many hadn't unpacked books and papers. Some sat talking quietly. Kyle Skillman methodically moved potato chips from bag to mouth. Others scribbled in notebooks—homework, letters, shopping lists. Some were reading, a few of them even reading Beckett or Joyce. Sally Mara was reading, too, but not *Molloy* or *Ulysses*. She was reading *The Old Man*.

Somehow I got through the hour. Somehow, talking about *Finnegans Wake*, *At Swim-Two-Birds* and early Beckett, and with several tactical detours to nearby Queneau country, I managed to keep them mostly awake and myself, if not exactly on track, then always within view of it, at least.

Sally Mara was waiting for me outside the classroom.

"Have a few minutes?" she asked. When I said I did, she fell in beside me, round face turned up as we walked.

"You'd look great with a beard," she said. We pushed our way through sluggish doors and started down the first half-flight of stairs. "Don't you think?"

"I had one once. Woman I was living with kept trying to grab it to do dishes, thought it was a Brillo pad."

Her smile broadened.

"You didn't tell us *you* were a writer, Mr. Griffin."

"Lots of things I don't admit to, Mrs. Mara. But somehow these nasty little secrets have a way of getting out."

"But you're *good*."

We started down the second half-flight.

"Thank you. But that was a long time ago. A different world."

"What are you working on now?"

For a moment I almost said, I'm trying to find my son.

"Nothing," I said instead.

By then we were at the office door. I put in the key and felt the entire lock assembly rotate as I turned it. I pushed at the cylinder with my other hand to hold it in place.

"That's . . . awful," Mrs. Mara said.

Finally got the door open.

"Sad," Mrs. Mara added.

Each year I feel the gap between myself and these young people widen—cracks taking over a floor as boards wear away. We don't live in the same world, hardly speak the same language. It's possible we never did. Though every year or so a face will tilt up out of some new mass of them, Conversational French or The Contemporary European Novel, yet another redundant student assembly, a group walking together down Magazine or in Lakeside Mall, and for a moment, as a kind of electric arc passes between us, I'll recognize: here is another.

Something of that sense now with Sally Mara.

"Not really," I told her. "There are probably too many books in the world already. And certainly too many second-rate writers."

She stood with one hip raised, leaning against the wall. Still smiling.

"I don't believe you mean that."

I remembered Dr. Lola Park as I said, "I'm sure you don't want to."

Using her other hip, Sally Mara pushed away from the wall. She came closer to me, inches away, face turned up, eyes searching mine.

"Then I won't."

Again, that sudden smile. There'd been times in my life I could have lived on that smile for months.

"I just wanted to thank you, Mr. Griffin. That's all. The course's been fabulous, I mean. But finding *your* books . . ."

She ducked her head.

"That's all, I just wanted you to know that."

"Thank you."

At the door she turned and said, all in a rush, "I think they're great Mr. Griffin. Really great!"

Then she was gone.

But today my dance card was full.

Another form replaced hers in the doorway. Light from the office's narrow, high window silhouetted his hair, like some exotic plant, on the wall behind.

"I waited outside. Had no desire to interrupt. Or to impose. Hope you don't mind."

He came a tentative step or two into the office.

Much more than that, of course, and he'd fetch up against the far wall.

"You remember me? Keith LeRoy?"

"Sure I do."

Last name accented on the first syllable. The young man with Woody Woodpecker hair who'd run Tast-T Donut all but single-handedly for minimum wage. Who, when I spoke to him on the phone, with his beeper and E-mail address, had glided so naturally from street talk to standard English.

"This where you work, huh."

I nodded.

"What you do."

Nodded again, then realized it was a question. I was nowhere near as sensitive as Keith LeRoy to inflection, to the subtle clues of class language. Though once I had been. So much gets lost along the way.

"I teach."

"Mmm-hmm," he said, looking around. "This all yours?"

"Pretty much."

"Good. That's good." Nodding. "What you teach."

"Literature. French."

"Parlez-vous and all that."

"Right."

"And literature."

"Novels. Stories. Essays. All the things people make up to try to understand and explain what we're doing here, what life's all about, why we choose the things we do."

"Mmm-hmm. You done this a long time."

"Keith, tell you the truth, it feels to me now like I've done *everything* a long time."

His topknot bobbed, directly before me and in silhouette on the wall behind, as he nodded.

"Know what you mean."

He looked about. At books and papers stacked on shelves behind my desk, at that narrow, high window, at the computer that worked when fate allowed, trays full of letters and interoffice memos.

"Always thought someday I might do this. Go this route. You know? Be a kick."

I don't think I even paused to consider his obvious intelligence, his easy, untutored shuttle among social stations. I simply said, "You decide to, let me know and I'll do whatever I can to help you. Since I'm teaching here, I have some voice in who gets admitted, who gets financial aid, that sort of thing."

He stood watching me.

"Really, man? Why would you want to do that for me?"

Hell if I knew.

"Any reason I shouldn't?"

He shook his head.

"Thanks," he said after a moment.

Maybe because I hadn't tried to help LaVerne, hadn't been able to help Alouette or my own son?

"Thank me after you decide and something comes of it."

He nodded. Seemed quite settled in there. Neither of us spoke for a couple of minutes.

"So . . ." he said.

"So."

"Few days ago you were looking for Shon Delany. That still up?"

"Till I find him, yeah."

"Figured. Well . . ."

That *well* went on and on, stretching taut like a clothesline, looping back on itself, suggesting all sorts of things. LeRoy had this way of squeezing a single word, *so*, *well*, for all it was worth.

" 'Round seven this morning my beeper goes off, and when I haul the body out of bed to a phone it's Delany on the other end, wondering when he can pick up his final check.

"I'm half an inch from telling him we don't *do* final checks—out of sight, out of mind, right? Invisible and insane, like the old joke goes— when I remember how you came 'round asking. So who knows why, but I decide to hold off, stall him. Told him maybe tomorrow. You got a number, I can call you then. I'll call *you*, he says. Right . . ."

Another verbal net thrown out. Dragging towards the boat, wriggling, sliding over one another's smooth bodies, a hearty catch of suppositions, implicit gestures, possibilities.

"How bad you want to talk to this Shon Delany?"

"His family asked me to find him."

"Family."

"Brother, actually. He's the one that takes care of them all. Shon's mother, some smaller kids."

"I used to have a brother, couple of years younger than me. Really smart. We all thought, this kid can do anything he wants to, anything at all. One Saturday night they shot him down in the parking lot outside Wal-Mart. Took him for someone else, maybe—or just drove by and he was there. We never knew. He'd just turned fourteen."

"I'm sorry."

"Yeah. Yeah, sure you are. Everyone is. Delany do something."

"I don't think so. Not yet."

"But you're thinking he hangs where he is, it's only a matter of time."

I nodded.

"Good kid."

"I know."

"But he has that hitch in his eye. Looking for something. Hungry."

I nodded again. Wondering if I had ever come across anyone, any age, who understood people the way Keith LeRoy did.

"Well. You are what you eat. Nothing larger than your own head, right?"

He smiled.

"Delany told me he had to have the money. Don't hold your breath, I said—anyway it's only a few dollars. He says, hole he's in, a few dollars could just make a difference."

LeRoy saw the question before I asked it. He shrugged.

"Who knows? That kind of need, it's got its own language."

"You think he'll call back?"

"I think he would of, yeah. But I told him I wouldn't be there—got my rounds to make, pickups and deliveries and the like. Be gone most of the day. Asked what part of town he was in, maybe we could meet up somewhere nearby later on. First he didn't answer. Then he said, 'I don't know . . .' "

Keith LeRoy grinned.

"You free 'round six o'clock, Mr. Griffin?"

"I could be."

"Good. Then you just might want to come along with me to the Funky Butt Bar, midcity. Have a sandwich, maybe a couple of beers, see what happens?"

Someone at the office door cleared his throat.

"I'll come by where you stay," Keith LeRoy said, "pick you up. That okay? 'Round five, five-thirty."

He nodded to me, then to my newest visitor, who stepped back out of the door to let him pass.

One last dance on my card, this time strictly ¼, a fox-trot, maybe.

Dean Treadwell wondered aloud just how serious was my dedication to teaching, to the university. He knew that I had a drinking problem, of course—and raised his hand when I started to protest. He understood, too, that my creative work, my own novels and stories, were of primary importance to me. He'd read and admired several of them himself, at his wife's urging. And devoted as it was to liberal arts, the university was happy to make certain concessions and accommodations. But.

Surely I understood that the university's obligation.

That the department must.

That I, as an untenured assistant professor, perhaps especially as an untenured assistant professor.

After all, we're all of us, students and faculty alike, on campus for.

Mind you, Treadwell's as fine a man as you're likely to pluck out from among these academic brambles and thickets. I'm sure he resented giving the lecture as much as I did receiving it.

So when he was done, I said "You're absolutely right" and handed over the office key. "You have to hold on to the lock, push in on it, to get it open. There's probably a trick to getting the computer to work too, but I haven't found it. The students pretty much take care of themselves."

"Mr. Griffin," he said. "Lewis. Please. Wait."

But I was in the doorway now, canceling out the rest of my dance card.

"I have been," I said. "Waiting. For far too long."

23

SO, NEWLY UNEMPLOYED, I lay on the couch belching beans and Crystal hot sauce, waiting for Keith LeRoy. Bat kept strafing the room: he'd dash in, jump on a rug and ride it across the floor till it crashed into wall or furniture, then retreat. I'd fed him, so this had to be some kind of higher complaint. Maybe he was afraid I'd no longer be able to provide for him in the manner to which he'd become accustomed.

I drifted as though on a raft: asleep, awake and somewhere in between, sounds around me settling in half-acknowledged, setting off sparks that caught at the dream-tinder.

Clare sat at the table by me. The sound of cars passing outside became her fingers on the keyboard. I'd just surfaced from a quart of gin, lying on the couch: she was home. Another review? Yes. It's going well? Fairly well, yes. Then, in the dream, I was again asleep.

Without transition I stood inside the ER doors, watching all those people rush towards Clare's room. White tile and bright light everywhere. Her overnight bag in my hand. Hairbrush and toothbrush, toothpaste, shampoo, one of the oversize T-shirts she wore to sleep in, all her usual meds.

Then in a dimly lit room I sat beside LaVerne as she poured martinis from a chilled pitcher, telling me about her childhood, her mother, and trains.

I looked up at her photo, the one Richard Garces gave me.

So many things I wanted to tell you, Verne.

I know.

I loved you more than any.

But with the same disabilities. Yes.

We can make up for our actions. But for our *in*actions, what we fail to do . . .

Do you think it's any different with me, Lew? With any of us? Let it go. This new woman you've met.

Deborah.

She makes you happy?

Yes.

Then cherish *her*, Lew. Tell *her* the things you never told me. Hold her close. And let her hold you.

I'll try. . . . Verne?

She was gone.

When I was a kid, twelve, thirteen, my father built a shoe-shine box for me. I'd said I wanted to earn my own money and a week later he handed me this thing. Solid hardwood box with a drawer for supplies, steel footrest above, a rod on the side for shoe-shine rags. Amazing piece of workmanship. He'd even stocked it with polishes, a brush, pieces of old towels. That Saturday he took me along on his usual rounds, Billy's D-light Diner, Cleburne Hotel Barber Shop, Blue Moon Tavern, DeSoto Park, and introduced me to his friends, many of whom, it happened, needed shoe-shines. I came home that day with almost eight dollars. I don't think I ever touched the box again. I spent the money on books. Paperbacks were a quarter back then. Seven dollars and change bought a lot of books. And earned a lot of grief from my mother, who for weeks complained of my wasting all that money, buying more books when I had a room full of them already.

When my own son was nine or ten, he asked for a magic cabinet. You'd put a ball in there, open doors and it would vanish, then you'd close and open the doors again and the ball would reappear. He'd come across the design for it in an old *Popular Mechanics* he found somewhere. So, calling upon what little I could remember of my father's skill, I built the cabinet for him, even painted on mysterious Chinese symbols. The cabinet sat on a shelf in his room for years, Janie told me, never used but always in clear sight.

"You comin' 'long or not?" Keith LeRoy said above me.

I looked up, for a moment disoriented.

"Let myself in, since you wouldn't answer the door. Hand got sore, standing out there knocking. You really oughta get a decent lock, man, you care about any of this shit."

I swung my legs over the side of the couch and sat up.

"Say that 'cause something for sure been goin' on 'round here, way there's eyes behind every window while I'm comin' down the street."

I told him about the juvenile muggers.

"Damn, they do be startin' early nowadays, don't they. So . . . You coming with?"

I came with.

Keith LeRoy led me to a dark green Mercedes parked in front of the house and when I looked at him questioningly told me, "Friend's car." He turned the key. The engine cleared its throat once, very discreetly, then was purring.

"Your friend takes good care of his car."

"Yeah. He's the kind takes care of *everything*. Business. Car."

"Friends."

"Yeah. 'Specially friends."

LeRoy signaled, watched in his wing mirror as he waited for a bread truck to pass, then pulled out. Went up Prytania to Jefferson, then left to Tchoupitoulas.

Twenty minutes later we were seated at a corner table near the door, me with coffee, looking up at the name painted in block white letters on the window outside, FUNKY BUTT, LeRoy with a draft beer, checking out two young ladies drinking margaritas at the bar. Paint had run between the final T's, making it look more like FUNKY BUM. I didn't know about the butt part, wasn't sure I wanted to know, but *funky* was dead on.

The bartender/waitress/cook, obviously a woman of many talents, dropped hamburgers on the table before us and stalked back towards the bar. Never know what might be going on up there while you were away. The hamburgers came in plastic baskets lined with waxed paper. Already grease was seeping through onto the tables.

I watched steam rise from the hamburger, grease spread below, as I finished my coffee. LeRoy downed his hamburger in four truly impressive bites. I'd just started mine when he said "There's your man" and stood.

He walked over to meet him. Neither made any move towards a handshake, anything like that, of course. They stood talking. Delany's eyes cut towards me.

It's not something you see too often on TV or in movies: the detective standing up with grease dribbling down his chin to apprehend a suspect.

I started for them just as Delany turned to leave. LeRoy's hand shot out and clamped on his upper arm.

That was when Armantine Rauch stepped through the door.

"Boy's with me," he said.

LeRoy looked once into Rauch's eyes and let go of Delany, stepping back, arms half-raised, palms out.

Rauch's eyes turned to me. We stood in mutual regard, no expression on our faces. Absolute quiet in the bar.

"We know one another?"

He must have seen something in my eyes like what LeRoy saw in his. A solid, compact little blue-steel .22 appeared.

"I sure as hell hope there ain't no goddamn heroes here."

The gun gave him confidence. Now his eyes could let go of mine. They swept the room. Shon Delany, still afraid to move. Keith LeRoy back against the wall. The girls at the bar, swiveled about to watch, skirts hiked high on their legs.

"Had about all I can stomach of heroes."

He smiled. Let the gun fall down along his leg.

"Man get a drink around here?"

"*Sure* you can, darlin'."

Rauch whirled about—and into the baseball bat that landed expertly just below the supraorbital ridge, at the bridge of his nose. He went back, and down, like a door slammed off its hinges, just as inert.

LeRoy lowered his hands. I picked up the .22, which slid towards me when Rauch fell. The girls swiveled back to the bar to slurp up the dregs of their drinks through pastel straws.

"Dam sonsabitches. Think they come in here and mess with *my* customers. Doan never learn." She laughed to herself. "Learned *him* anyways."

As I said, a lady of many talents. First sign of trouble, she'd gone out the back door and around. With her Louisville slugger.

Not a game I much care for, baseball, but it has its points.

Bartender/waitress/cook/enforcer, she stepped behind the bar again and announced: "Last call, ladies and gentlemen. Might want to order doubles. Cops be here soon enough."

I knew just what she meant.

All *kinds* of undesirables dropping by this afternoon.

24

"WHO'S THE CIVILIAN?" an officer standing by the door wanted to know. Dressed like that, shiny, salmon-colored polyester suit, short-sleeve white shirt, narrow tie short enough to show the straining button just above his belt, nothing else he could be.

Don looked at him and after a moment, shifting his gaze to the floor, shook his head.

"You hear anyone else in here interrupting me, DeSalle?"

DeSalle grunted.

"You know why that is?"

No response this time.

"It's because they've all acquired your basic manners, DeSalle. Civility. Even *this* shitbag."

Don gestured towards Rauch.

"Sticks screwdrivers in old men, knocks off a couple of friends, who knows what else he does in his spare time. But you'll notice *he* doesn't interrupt me.

"As for Lew here, he's directly involved. He's also a guest of the senior officer, here by request. Don't guess you have *your* invitation there in your pocket, do you?"

Again no response from DeSalle.

"So. We straight on this?"

After a moment the officer nodded.

"Thing is," Don went on, talking now to Armantine Rauch, "we're willing to overlook a lot of things. Have to, all that goes on around here, limited manpower we have."

Don shook his head and leaned closer over the table. Two men in the same business, you might as well say, comparing notes.

"Bodies are different, Rauch. We don't get away with overlooking those for long. Mayor's office, citizens' groups, the paper, TV shows calling us America's murder capital and pushing for federal investigations. Everybody's got a list. And when those lists start getting too long they just naturally get louder and louder about it. Hey, you want some coffee or something? A cigarette?"

Rauch shook his head.

"You sure? Okay, just let me know if you change your mind. So what you think? You think you might be able to help me with this?"

Rauch smiled.

"Your men took my wallet."

"Sorry: regulations."

"My lawyer's card is in there. Maybe *he*'ll be able to help you."

Don nodded. "You're probably right. Probably save me a lot of time and effort. Lawyers usually do, bless them. Officer DeSalle?"

"Yessir."

"Will you please go check and be sure this man's lawyer has been notified?"

We all sat looking at one another until DeSalle returned.

"Call's been made," he said.

"Then we're just having a quiet talk while we wait, in the spirit of cooperation, am I right?" Don asked.

"I don't believe my lawyer would want me to say anything until he arrives."

"Yeah. Yeah, I'm sure you're right."

There was a knock at the door. A uniform poked his head through to talk to DeSalle, then withdrew.

DeSalle passed it along: "Counselor Silberman—that's Mr. Rauch's lawyer, Lieutenant—is currently unavailable. Seems he's on vacation in Barbados for a couple weeks."

"Well," Don said. "That does present us with something of a problem, doesn't it, Rauch? We can petition for a court-appointed lawyer, some kid just out of law school or some burned-out case carrying twice as many cases as anyone could possibly handle."

"Or you can hold me over till such time as my own attorney becomes available."

"Good take on the situation," Don said.

"Thank you."

"Listen, you mind waiting here a few minutes? Couple things I've gotta take care of."

DeSalle and I followed Don out of the room.

"We really try calling that shitbag's lawyer?" he asked.

"This time, I didn't make it up. Didn't have to. Guy's really in Barbados."

"Not much room to maneuver there, then."

"Not much."

"So now I guess we hit number two and hope he really does try harder, see if we can jump-start *him*."

Shon Delany was in the next room, seated behind a high, desk-sized table. They'd put a canned Coke, a cellophane-shrouded sandwich from a vending machine, a pack of Salems and a Bic lighter on the table. Delany was drinking the Coke.

Don introduced himself and asked if there was anything else he could get.

"You want another Coke, maybe? some ice? a slice of pizza?

"No?

"Look, son, I'm not supposed to—my superiors find out, I'm in for a major ass-chewing—but I feel like I have to tell you this. Your buddy in there rolled over on you. Told us about the burglaries and all the rest. Names, dates, details. What you did with the take."

"But I don't know about any of that."

"Well. Sure you don't. But . . ."

Don spread his hands imploringly as DeSalle stepped forward.

"I'll *but* him," DeSalle said.

Don smiled. "See what I mean? Day comes to an end, folks like yourself shoved in here, all this paperwork, I've just naturally got to have some kind of answers for the people upstairs."

"But I don't *know* anything," Delany said. "I'd help you if I could."

"I'm sure you would. So for a start why don't you tell us why you killed Daryl Anthony Payne."

"What?"

"Come *on*, Delany. Rauch told us all about it. How he begged you to stop, let it go, but you wouldn't. Out of control, he said. Totally OOC."

"Wait a minute, okay? I didn't *kill* anyone."

"You think that matters, Shon? The meter's ticking. I gotta draw a line at the bottom, add it all up, column A, column B. That's what the city and the citizens pay me for. And my wife's expecting me home for dinner.

"You saw anything maybe you weren't supposed to see, something that could put this in a different light for us, now's your time to lay it on the table."

"Only chance you'll get," DeSalle echoed.

"He's right. I don't blow smoke, Shon. We're doing our best here, trying to be up front with you. Your cousin's going down. Up to you whether he drags you down with him or not."

"You need paper and a pen?" DeSalle said. "Want to write it all down for us?"

Shon Delany shook his head.

"Okay, Shon," Don said. "Okay. I understand. DeSalle?"

"Yessir?"

"You want to drop the dime on this young man for me? Just tell County we've got a new fish for them, they want to bring the hooks, come get him."

"Look, I do get to make a phone call, right?" Delany said.

Don looked surprised.

"Man hasn't had his call yet? How'd *that* happen?"

"I'm not sure, sir. I'll look into it."

"You do that, Detective. But first you take Mr. Delany into my office, let him use my phone."

"Yessir."

"*Then* you call County. And me, at home, to let me know it's all been taken care of. Pot roast tonight. Should be coming out of the oven just about now. I don't want to miss it."

DeSalle and Shon Delany left.

"Pot roast, huh?" I said. "And a wife."

"Not bad, huh? Maybe *I* should start writing novels. What can I say? Attitude's everything."

Don looked up at the clock on the wall opposite the interrogation rooms.

"Don't guess you want to grab some dinner this late?"

"Why not. What the hell, I might even spring for it."

"Whoa . . . Scary."

Don glanced back at the clock. We both knew he didn't want to go home.

"Give me a minute or two, okay, Lew? Meet you outside."

"Sad thing is," he said half an hour later, as we settled back in a booth at a hole-in-the-wall named Tony's, one of Don's favorites, "the kid, Delany, he's probably gonna take a hit for this. A small hit, but a real one. Got a sheet now, carry it around for the rest of his life. Never did crapola, probably doesn't have even half a clue. While this *other* shit, just because he knows the system, he'll get all the breaks."

A huge platter of oysters cruised into port before us.

"Thanks, Tony," Don said.

"You gonna work on these awhile?"

"You better believe it."

"Want another beer?"

Don said yes. He got it instantly.

"You want anything else, just let me know, right?"

"Right."

Tony disappeared into the kitchen. We heard rapid-fire chopping back there.

"You still seeing this O'Neil person?" Don asked. He loaded horse-radish onto an oyster, forked the whole thing into his mouth.

I nodded.

"Things going all right there?"

Cocktail sauce this time. Another Rabelaisian swallow.

And I nodded.

"Good. That's good, Lew. Happy for you."

Don drained off half his beer in a gulp.

"Maybe we could get together, just the three of us, have dinner some night."

"I'd like that."

"Yeah. Yeah, I would too."

He poured the rest of his beer down.

"We'll work on that, then."

Tony emerged from the kitchen to slide another beer into place before

Don and to refill my glass of iced tea, pouring sideways from the pitcher, just as Don's beeper went off.

He pulled it off his belt, put it on the table and stared at it.

"Maybe I should just shoot the damned thing."

"Probably go down okay, you put enough horseradish on it."

"Yeah."

Don stalked off towards the phone booth.

"Ready for menus?" Tony asked.

"Remains to be seen."

"As usual. I'll just leave them here on the table then, check back with you."

"Sounds good."

"Today's soup is cream of artichoke. Specials are trout in garlic sauce and penne pasta alfredo with grilled shrimp. Either one's guaranteed to leave you drooling into next Tuesday."

"Thanks, Tony. I'm drooling already."

"No problem. Need an extra napkin?"

"Not yet. But some more tea would be great, when you get a chance."

"You got it."

Don came back and sank heavily into the booth across from me.

"Guess you have a big night planned, right, Lew? With your new girl and all."

"Not really."

"You mind coming with me, then? I could use the company."

He stood and tucked a five under the saltshaker.

"Sure. Where we going?"

"It's Danny, Lew. They just found him. Place down on Dryades. Apparent suicide."

25

DANNY WAS HALF afloat, half submerged, in a tubful of tepid water. One of those old tubs, heavy as a kettle, up off the ground on a platform, with clawed feet. A garbage bag around his head was tied at the neck. His tongue, swollen and purple, protruded. Blood vessels in his eyes had burst, making them look like road maps with nothing but interstates. Bladder and bowels had let go in the water.

DeSalle stepped up behind Don. He didn't speak till Don turned around.

"Looks like an overdose, with the bag for insurance. One of the uniforms told me there's a society recommends this route."

"Who took the call?" Don said.

"Patrolman you mean?"

"Yeah."

"Martinez. Young guy. Pretty new, I guess, taking it hard the way we all do the first few times."

"He out there?" Don gestured towards the front room.

"Yeah. Thought you might want to talk to him yourself."

"Anybody else around?"

DeSalle shook his head. "Have been, though. Two, three people at least living here, looks like. Maybe more."

"Note?"

DeSalle handed it to him. Sheathed in a sleeve of clear plastic with DeSalle's initials scrawled across the seal. There was only one light in the room, a bare bulb above the sink. Don stood under it as he read the note. Then he passed the note to me.

> It all comes down to choice, doesn't it? The ones we have, the ones we don't have. Those we make and those we're never able to make. Temporary choices, inadvertent choices, final choices.
>
> Fuck them all. While I'm at it, fuck your goddamn houses out in Metairie and your kids in private schools, fuck your minimum-wage jobs, your sorry-ass unions.
>
> Fuck your cops most of all.
>
> Am I making myself clear here?
>
> Everything's water if you look long enough, right?

"It's a strange one," DeSalle said.

I handed the note back to Don. "No heading or salutation."

"Right."

"Left side's ragged. Torn out of a notebook, diary, something like that."

DeSalle looked from Don to me and back.

"Something I missed?"

"Lew's just saying the note's not addressed to anyone."

"Hell it's not."

"Yeah," Don said after a moment. "Yeah, you're right. Guess any list would have been too long. Boy had a lot of anger in him. Always thought it was *other* people fucked up his life."

Don stepped into the front room to speak with Martinez.

"You guys go back a way, huh?"

I told DeSalle how Don and I met. Both of us little more than kids, each with his own reason to be searching for the sniper that killed all those people back in the sixties.

"Damn, Griffin. That was *you*?"

Don had been shot by the sniper. I'd come upon them in a downtown cul-de-sac and probably saved Don's life—at least he insisted I had. Since then he'd saved mine more times than I could count.

"Not many like him on the force," DeSalle said.

"Not many like him anywhere."

"You know it. Has to be tough," looking at Danny there in the tub, "all this."

"Can't imagine anything tougher. But I think he'd been getting ready for it, something like this."

"Yeah. Lives with it every day. Has to know."

"For a long time now."

Then forensics was upon us.

Tape measures chirred, whisk brooms and tiny vacuums whispered, bits of debris tumbled into baggies. Again and again our shadows struck huge on the walls as flashes went off.

Don stood at the edge of it all, just outside the doorway, watching.

Also there, wheezing like a bad accordion, sucking alternately at metered-dose inhalers of Atrovent or Albuterol and oxygen from the portable compressor hung like an oversize binocular case under one arm, directing auteurlike this too-real dramatic moment, stood Dr. Bijur.

"Your boy, I understand."

"Yeah."

She shook her head. Squeezed off two hits of Ventolin then wheezed a long exhale.

"Sure it's top of the list for you. For me it's just one more, pick a number, twelve, thirteen, in there. Wait your turn."

"I say anything?"

"You will."

Her shoulders lifted with the effort to drag more air into faltering lungs.

"Do the same myself in your position, Walsh. No way I wouldn't. King's horses couldn't stop me."

"Special favors aren't an option here, Sonja. Okay. But I *would* appreciate anything you can give me quick."

What she gave him was a fit of coughing. Sounded as though nails and planks were being ripped out of her body's floor.

Don waited for her to recover.

"City lets me have half the personnel I need with twice the workload I can handle. Not a good match, Walsh."

"I know something about that myself."

"My department's response time is half that of L.A., beats out New York, Boston, Baltimore, and D.C. by several wide miles. Our reports hit your desk within twenty-four hours. Thirty-six at the outside. You ever got your head out of this city's ass long enough to look around, you could probably work up some pride in that."

Again, coughs racked her. She cranked up the O's from 2 L/M to 4.

"You know what it'll take, right? Some young sport's gonna come in here once I'm gone. Wear a tie to work every day, have nice letterhead, maybe an MBA. That's the new thing."

"Yeah. Yeah, we got them coming up that way through the force now too. Straight off the streets and into offices with espresso machines."

"Reports are gonna get slower and slower. They'll also get increasingly worthless as the M-B-Assholes worry about covering their own butts above all, to hell with evidence, fact, inference, extrapolation."

Dr. Bijur dosed herself with Atrovent, inhaling the puff and holding it like a hit of marijuana, talking around it.

"We been. At this. A while now. Haven't we?"

"We have indeed, Sonja."

Another long exhalation.

"Bumpy road. Lots of lows. A few highs."

"Few enough."

"Truly sorry about this one, Walsh."

Our shadows leapt on the walls again.

"Never had a family myself. Doesn't mean I don't know what it's like."

"Yeah."

"You're a better cop than you ever were a father."

"Being a cop's easy."

"Yeah. I guess." Words came in a rush, breathless, high in her chest. barely heard the last few. "You—"

Her mouth went on moving but no words came forth. Her face turned dark.

"Sonja? You okay? Want me to call the paramedics?"

"No . . . no. I'm, okay. Give me. A minute."

It took more than a minute, but gradually her breathing eased, her color improved.

By then her technicians had finished and came to tell her so.

She looked at Don.

"Guess we're packing it up. Both have to get back to work now, huh? The *real* work."

"Looks like it."

"No more time for flirting."

"Flirting. Now, there's a word I haven't heard in a while. My God, are we really that old, Sonja?"

"How'd it happen, huh? I know. I wonder myself. Things go on, years pile up. All the lists get longer."

He stood watching her go.

"Lew," Don said.

"Yeah."

"Okay if I stay with you tonight?"

"Absolutely."

26

"DAMN. ANOTHER MOUTH to feed," Zeke said. He'd passed by Don, asleep on the couch, on his way into the kitchen where I sat drinking coffee, wondering how early I could start making calls: Sam Delany to tell him I'd found his brother, Keith LeRoy to thank him for his help, Deborah.

Zeke poured himself a cup and sat down across from me. Sniffed at it and held on with both hands, huddling over it the way cons do.

"I was worried about you," I told him. "Haven't seen you in a few days."

"Well, I been working on something, just steady chippin' away at it. You know how that is."

"Getting anywhere?"

Zeke shrugged. "Hard to say. We can talk about it later. Meantime, that cop draped all over your couch out there's gotta be your friend Walsh." He'd know instantly, of course, that Don was a cop. No surprise there. "What's up?"

I told him about Danny. Zeke's eyes narrowed when I described the bathroom scene, but he said nothing.

Afterwards he shook his head and poured us each another cup.

"Guess I'd best be puttin' together some breakfast."

"Thanks, Zeke. We could probably all use it."

"The two of you could for sure. *I've* got to scoot on out of here." At my glance he held up an admonitory hand. "Told you. Talk about it later."

He carried his coffee to the counter, began pulling out eggs, bread, onions, a potato.

"Fifteen minutes," he said. "Meanwhile, you go start excavating the pharaoh. Oh, and Lewis?"

"Yeah."

"You might want to give some thought to checking your messages ever' week or so. Last I counted, there were a stone dozen of them out there on the machine. How long they had those things out, anyway?" Chopping onions, he shook his head. "What *else* they goan come up with?"

Don proved a most reluctant pharaoh, starting up instantly, wild-eyed, when I first approached, settling back at once into shadowy, encumbered sleep. I poked at him, shouted, passed steaming coffee under his nose. Finally levered him up and out to the kitchen, where Zeke had filled the table with food. Don ate, drank most of a pot of coffee and shambled back to the couch. Zeke left to be about his business. I did dishes and sat staring at the blinking light on the phone machine.

This is one of the ways our past finds us. Dots we connect to make a shape on the white page.

First was Deborah: "Hey, big boy. Remember me?"

Two and three were from the university. Please call.

Four was Sam Delany.

The next couple, I don't know *what* they were. People didn't seem to have much idea who they were calling but left rambling, incomprehensible messages nonetheless.

Seven was Deborah again: "Guess not."

Then another from Dean Treadwell's office, someone offering me a bank card, an old client from my PI days wondering if I'd be able to help him again, my agent saying there'd been a Hollywood nibble on one of my books and how was I these days, a couple more junk calls.

I dialed the flower shop.

"Rumors of my death, and all that," I said when Deborah answered.

"Lew! Everything okay?"

I told her about finding Shon Delany, then about Don's son.

"I'm so sorry, Lew. How's Don?"

"Tough, as always."

"Sounds like you've had a couple of tough days yourself."

"I distinctly remember easier ones."

"Don't we all. When can I see you?"

"This point, I don't have a clue what the day's likely to turn into. Not another grade-A mess like yesterday is what I hope. Okay if I call you later?"

"Sure it is. Or just come by."

"Right."

I took the last of the coffee out back, sat on the wooden bench layered with bird droppings under the tree out there. The bench's underside was a thicket of crumbling leaves and spiderwebs. Been years since I last did this. LaVerne and I spent a lot of time on that bench. Go out there late at night, take glasses of wine out while dinner simmered on the stove, coffee first thing in the morning.

I'd sat out here like this the morning I learned of David's disappearance. Later I'd written that a toad had jumped into my face, but the toad was becoming only history, and bearable.

Through the kitchen window I heard the radio playing. Wagner's overture to *The Flying Dutchman*, whose questionable hero the devil overhears saying he'll round the cape if it takes forever and decides to take at his word, turning him into a marine version of Sisyphus. An equally questionable angel intervenes, doling him out one day every seven years on dry land, telling the Dutchman he can be released from this if only he's able to find a woman who'll follow him into death.

Much like that questionable hero or angel, Don appeared in the doorway.

"Tell me it's still Tuesday."

"Yep. Ticking away like all the rest of them. Time goes, we stay."

"What time?"

"Around eleven, I think. I called the department, told DeSalle you wouldn't be in. He said no problem, no one expected you to be. Wanted me to let you know he was thinking about you."

"Good man."

"You could be right about that."

Don nodded and dropped onto the bench beside me. For a long time he sat vaguely looking off at the house's back wall. The wall was covered in green, runners and vines that had started inching up it years ago. Chameleons darted in and out among them.

I had no idea what thoughts were turning, surfacing, sinking back down in Don's mind. When do we ever, however close we are to someone?

"Lot of years between us," he finally said.

I nodded.

"Lot of horses shot out from under us. Both of us."

"No doubt about it. But we always managed to get up again and walk on."

After a moment he said, "Maybe there were times we shouldn't have."

The Flying Dutchman ended. The phone rang. I listened for the message and couldn't make it out. I put my hand atop my friend's. He looked down at them together there on the bench as though they were some new kind of life he hadn't seen before, something strange and ultimately unknowable, generated from the muck and silt of leaves below, maybe.

"I've been telling you for a while now that it was time you actually *found* someone—one of these people you're forever looking for."

"Yeah. And I always said you were probably right."

"Now I'm thinking maybe that someone should be David."

We sat watching vines and runners that didn't move, chameleons that didn't stop. Inside, the phone rang again. Don's beeper went off.

"Together, I mean. We could look for him together. I have a lot of time coming to me."

When I didn't respond, he said, "We did it before, Lew."

We had indeed. The way we met. And how often in all the years since? Too many to count.

"Maybe it's time we did that again, Lew."

Maybe it was.

I nodded.

"Good," my friend said. "Good."

27

It was good, having old friends greet me. They all stood at the doors of their cells watching. A few of them nodded. I walked down the wide corridor, between the high tiers. Behind Stanley, who used to tell me about his kids and the old Dodge he barely kept running. I was thinking how all my life I never felt I belonged anywhere. Now I knew I did. I belonged here.

I HIT SAVE, backed the last twenty or so pages onto a disk to join the rest, then started a printout.

My letter to Vicky, which had turned into a reinvention of *The Old Man*, then into a memoir of LaVerne, later into some Cocteauesque fantasy of men in black tuxedos and women in white dresses emerging from cave mouths or subways, had resolved with absolute simplicity, in a matter of twelve or fourteen intense, ever-surprising hours, into a sequel to my prison novel, *Mole*.

I woke on the floor.

The printer had stopped for lack of paper. The phone had stopped too—a couple of times at least, I realized. But now it was ringing again.

"You there?" Walsh said when I picked up. "Hello? Intelligent life?"

"Semi, anyway. Listen, Don, I haven't got any sleep yet. Not so you'd notice it, anyway. You want to call me back later?"

"Sure I do. Guess I'll have to, to get your sorry ass off the dime. But if you haven't been sleeping, then just what the hell is it you *have* been doing?"

"I'm as surprised as you are, believe me—but I guess I've just finished a new book."

"A new book. Another book. No hope for you, is there, Lew? I leave you alone for just a few hours—I mean, I figure this is safe, we'll both grab some sleep, get out there and take care of business—but no. *You* decide to spend your time on a book."

"Just what my mother used to say. Only then it was reading books, not writing them."

"Yeah, you told me. Also told me your mother was flat-out bonkers. So." Don paused—to drink coffee, from the sound of it. "This a good one?"

"Never sure at first. I *think* it is."

Don made an ambiguous sound somewhere between grunt and laugh. "Call me when you're back up to speed?"

"Half-speed may be the best I'll manage for a while."

"Know what you mean. Good enough, though."

"You at home?"

"Yeah."

"And?"

He knew what I was asking. That's the thing about old friends. So many of your most important conversations are silent.

"It's gonna take time, Lew. But listen."

"Yeah?"

"DeSalle called. Rauch is gonna walk. We scrambled, but there's no way we can make a hard enough case to get him bound over, everything circumstantial like it is. So we have him on disorderly and possession and that's about it. We could hold on to him for another twenty-four to forty-eight hours, but what's the point? You see any?"

"Guess not. What about Delany?"

"Back in the bosom of his family even as we speak."

Guess that was one phone call I'd waited too long to make.

"Thanks, Don."

"Lights out, then. You want, I could sing you a lullaby."

"Not at this point in time."

"Right. Well, I offered."

I loaded the printer with paper, hit Retry and heard it hum into action. Page 52 rolled into the tray. Short book. Publisher'd have to leave lots of space everywhere: borders, margins, between lines and chapters.

Obviously, at some threshold of concern the book's length was gnawing at me. And I had learned to listen to those promptings.

Maybe the book wasn't a sequel at all.

Maybe it was just the second half of *Mole*—the part I hadn't told before.

There was no clock in the slave quarters, so I walked back over to the house. Bat met me at the door, complaining emphatically. Obviously I was a great disappointment. He'd put so much time into training me. And here I couldn't get the simplest, basic things right.

I opened a can of food and put it on the floor.

Almost eight. I might still be able to catch Deborah at home.

"How's the fatted calf?" I said when she answered.

"Fatter and fatter. I, on the other hand, just got out of the shower and am dripping all over. Have a carpet of mold here by the phone by tomorrow morning. Call you back?"

"Sure."

"Me," she said when I answered five minutes later.

"Dry?"

She thought about it. "That a leading question?"

Then she laughed, and I thought how much I treasured that laugh, how much I read into it.

"Words *will* go on meaning what they want to, won't they? Hard as we try to control them."

"Need a few good sheepdogs. Like those you told me about at the Celtic festival out in Kenner."

Four of them, each a different breed, each trained to cues in a different language. Only took a word or two from the master. An amazing display. Closest thing to perfect communication I'd ever seen.

"Exactly. But I think in this case *we're* supposed to be the sheepdogs, Lew."

"Unacknowledged legislators of the world."

"Forging blah-blah in the smithy of our soul and so on. Oh yeah. Though my own experience tells me it's a lot more like disaster control."

Bat had finished his food but continued nosing the can around the kitchen floor, fetching it up against cabinets, refrigerator, stove and screen door in some deathless dream of extracting a few final morsels.

I apologized to Deborah for not calling or coming by as I'd said I would, then told her about the new book. I guess it was a book. More like a patchwork quilt for me at this point. I remembered individual pages, scenes, all these small islands, couldn't make much sense of the whole thing.

"But that's *great*, Lew."

"I guess. Right now I feel like a truck ran over me, braked, and backed up to have another go just in case."

"So get some sleep, call me later."

"Déjà vu time, huh."

"Yeah, well. Most of our lives are strictly top-forty. Same songs over and over."

"Some comfort in that."

"And lots of ho-hum."

But somehow ho-hum didn't seem the enemy it once did. All Bat asked of life was that it be predictable, ordered. Furniture, litter box, food and water dish where they were supposed to be, meals at eight and five, no surprises. Maybe Bat had the right idea.

I was pretty sure Sam Delany did.

The phone rang moments after Deborah and I hung up. He was calling to thank me, he said. Didn't know if I could ever understand how much this meant to him. To all the family. Please send a bill for my services and expect his check by return mail.

"One more thing," Delany told me.

"Yes?"

"My mother said for me to tell you God bless, for bringing her son back to her."

"You tell her I appreciate that, Sam."

"Yessir. Yessir, I will."

I poured O'Doul's into a glass, took it out to the slave quarters and began sorting pages. Forty, maybe fifty to go. They curled up slowly, swaybacked, out of the belly of the machine and wherever they'd come from before that, into the world.

What I needed was a *real* drink.

I went back into the house, stuffed my wallet into my shorts and made for the K&B on St. Charles, one block over, six down, where I stood in line behind a well-sweated bus driver buying five bags of cookies, two kids with vaguely Celtic tattoos at ankle, bicep and shoulder and with multiple rings (ear, lip, brow) clinging to them, an elderly black man ensconced in beautifully pressed and appointed dress clothes fifty years out of date.

Abita, as it happened, was on sale. I emerged with a six-pack of Amber in a doubled plastic bag. Walked back over to Prytania with the old man while he told me about his life as a streetcar driver, how much the city and its people had changed over the years. Then we turned different directions, uptown, downtown.

But I wasn't alone. A bicycle shot by. Half a block and three minutes later it circled back, looping past more slowly. Two riders. Young black men. Apparently tracking a woman who'd stepped out of one of the nearby stand of newly restored doubles on her way to car and work.

No reason to worry about me. Poorly dressed old black man, unshaven, unkempt, shuffling along with his morning beer. Hardly likely to cause problems. Be gone the instant anything happened.

I stepped up my pace until I was close upon her, crossed Toledano mere steps behind. I'd begun swinging the six-pack in its plastic bag idly at my side, letting the arc grow. Concerned about my encroachment, unaware of the real danger, the woman walked faster.

No sound of traffic anywhere nearby.

That's when they came sailing in.

That's also when I spun around, letting the bag fly out, adding the force of my turn to its own weight and momentum.

It struck the driver full in the face. He fell heavily back, dislodging his passenger, and the three of them, driver, passenger and bike, went skidding beneath a jacked-up pickup parked half a block down. Several bottles of Abita, whole and partial, chattered against the curb.

The woman who'd been their target turned abruptly towards St. Charles.

The driver was dead out, with a broken nose and a face that in a day or so would be one massive, masklike bruise. Beneath oversize shorts worn low on his hips, the passenger's tibia jutted out through the flesh of his leg. Neither of them was going anywhere.

I knocked at the nearest house and when a lady in pink housecoat and slippers let the door out on its chain, asked if she'd mind calling the police. She looked off at the kids under the truck, nodded, and, backing away, shut and locked the door.

28

D O W E E V E R know how much of what we do, what we decide, what we set in motion, is conscious, how much purely not?

Easy now to look back at walking away from the university, at my activities over the next several days, even at the new book with its protagonist's acceptance of his apartness and withdrawal, and see the pattern.

As always we go on living our lives forward, attempting to understand them backwards.

Later that day the unofficial neighborhood watch captains, Norm Marcus and son Raymond, Gene and Janet Prue, came to thank me for putting an end to the robberies. My disavowals and claim that I'd only been on an errand, minding my own business, they refused to accept as other than becoming modesty. After all, they watched TV; they knew how Mannix, Rockford and all my other colleagues occupied themselves. Obviously I'd been out doing legwork, figured where and when the kids were likely to strike next and contrived to be there. Good detectives make good neighbors.

Eventually I managed to shoehorn them out. All but Raymond, who lingered behind.

"Something I can do for you, Raymond?"

"Ray. That's what most everyone calls me 'cept family. Others call me RM."

"Okay. Ray it is."

"Writing a term paper on those sniper shootings back in the sixties, Carl Joseph, all that. Wondered if you might be able to help me some with it."

Thinking the intruders gone, Bat sauntered back into the room and saw Ray. He reversed in mid-step, picking up speed the whole time, and skittered away, barely making the corner.

"Lew," I told the boy. "That's what everyone calls me."

He nodded. "Know you're busy."

"Not *that* busy. You come on over whenever you want to, we'll talk about all that."

"Thanks . . . Lew."

He held out his hand. My God, I thought, you wait long enough, they *do* turn into human beings. Some of them, anyway.

I spent the next hour or so, figuratively, making lists. Not that I'm by nature a list maker. Tend to improvise, I guess: books, days, life. My mother, on the other hand, was a champion. Her whole life was a list. And for *most* of her life it wasn't much more. Her clock was set at 5:15. The coffeepot came on at 5:00. She left for work at 7:52. Dinner—until after the old man died and, alone, she gave up dinners, pretty much gave up eating at all, living on coffee and cigarettes—was at 6:00.

Saturdays she cleaned house, beginning with the bathroom, finishing up with the kitchen. Every Sunday she listened to church services on the radio, read her magazines, wrote letters. Even the letters read like lists.

(Where was my father in all this? Out in his workshop, I guess. He spent more and more time there as years went by. Years ago, when Mom died, I tried to talk to my sister Francy about this. What was going on between them? What happened? What was wrong with her? What did he think about out there? Francy would only shrug.)

Wanting to be sure she'd received the new manuscript, I called my agent. Marlene was on another line, but her secretary confirmed that not only did they have the novel, they'd already sent it out. Had even had a nibble or two, though no strikes. Did I want to hold? No. And it might be a while before I was in touch again.

Next I rang Dean Treadwell's office to say that yes I had resigned my position and no I did not foresee returning, nor did I have reason to speak personally with the dean.

I began sorting through bills I kept in a basket on the kitchen table. Wrote checks to pay everything off in full: credit cards (American Express,

Citibank Visa, Dillard's, Sears), Maple Street Book Store, South Central Bell, NOPSI. Sent the mortgage company a check covering the next year. Then put all the rest away in a drawer and picked up the phone again.

Dialed one number and when I got no response, dialed another.

"Yeah?"

"Don there?"

"Walsh?"

"How many Dons you have?"

"Thought maybe you were calling up the Mob. You know?" At least he spared me the Brando imitation. "This Griffin?"

"Yeah. No anonymity in the electronic age, huh."

"How hard could it be? You're the only friend he has."

"DeSalle?"

"You bet."

"What the hell'd *you* do, they've got you answering phones?"

"You think they tell us anything down here? Mushrooms, right? City's cutting back. Casinos didn't hump it quite the way council members thought, didn't bail the city out. Some goddamn surprise. So now we've got a few million in new debts and an abandoned shell up there on Basin that'll be around well past the millennium. I hang up, for all I know my next assignment's cleaning bathrooms. Talk about your sense of history.

"Hang on, Lew," he told me. Then, raising his voice: "Hey, Walsh. You taking calls today or what?"

A brief reply I couldn't make out.

"You wish."

This time a longer reply.

"Yeah, but she wasn't *that* good." Back to me: "He's here. He's live." Turning away again: "Yo. Walsh. Hello?" To me: "Hold on. May have got his attention." Then: "It's Griffin. You want to talk to him or not? No one else will."

"Lew."

"Enjoying your time off, I see."

"Hey. Officially I'm not even here. Just figured since you were gonna be out of frame for a while, I might as well use the time to catch up on paperwork. What else am I gonna do? Lay sod in the backyard?"

I didn't say anything.

"You start whistling that 'Don't Worry, Be Happy' thing, I'll have to come over there and kick butt."

We sat listening to the hum in the wires.

"Lew?"

"Yeah."

"What's going on?"

After a moment I said, "I'm not sure."

"Have to tell you I don't much like the sound of that."

"Wouldn't expect you to. Not too crazy about it myself, all things considered." Leaves had gone dead still outside my window. "I may be away for a while, Don."

"I see. We talking a long while or a short one here?"

"I don't know that either."

"Okay."

Wind started up again. Had waited, coiled in the trees, till now. Windows chattered in their panes. Strands of Spanish moss blew sideways. A few let go. The sky grew dark.

"You know where I am."

Yes.

"Call me."

I said I would. A stutter of rain started down outside.

"Take care, Lew."

Deborah would be at work, of course. I left a message on her home machine, asking if she'd take care of Bat, telling her I'd leave a key with Norm Marcus down the street, just in case Zeke wasn't around when she came by. I waited, wanting to say something else, getting ready to, but before I could, the machine cut off.

I went into the kitchen to put a message on the refrigerator door for Zeke and stood there looking out the window above the sink. Rain fell without sound through the trees.

So much of my life bound up with this house. So many mornings and evenings and nights I'd stood here just like this, or sat at the table for long hours with LaVerne, Don, Alouette. Quiet moments as the world outside whirled past, over and around.

Just as it did now.

For by this time the storm had arrived in earnest and incontrovertibly. Rain streamed off roof's edge, a solid curtain, shutting off that world, leaving me marooned here on this mutable island.

Such comfort, such misgiving, in it.

29

Sometimes the future dwells in us without our knowing it and when we think we are lying our words foretell an imminent reality.

PROUST, OF COURSE.

30

SO IT IS that my own Nighttown sequence begins.

Waiting only for the storm to subside, wearing old green jeans I usually reserved for yard work, a pair of blue-and-silver swayback knockoff Nikes, bruise-purple flannel shirt over a denim shirt faded almost to white and a well-worn, well-torn red T-shirt, green bandanna tied at my neck, I left the house within hours of speaking to Don and leaving the message for Deborah. Instinctively I headed for the river. I looked like Doo-Wop at a fashion show.

If indeed there's something at our centers, how do we find our way to it? The doors that should lead there open into closets and storage places, onto dead corridors, back to the outside.

All our lives, every day, we constantly remake ourselves, reinvent ourselves, layer after layer, mask after mask. Maybe when finally we peel off all the masks there's nothing left. Maybe Doo-Wop in his own timeless way is right: we're nothing but the stories we tell ourselves and others.

I remembered, years ago, walking just like this by the levee downtown, smelling automobile exhausts, stagnant water and all the things that grow in it, hops and yeast from the old Jax brewery. I'd just been sprung from a long, court-enforced hospital stay, locked doors, locked razors. No home, no work or career left, just trunks full of loose connections. That day the terms *tabula rasa* and *palimpsest* had drifted into my mind.

I also remembered, further back, waking up at the base of that same levee after a night's hard drinking with bluesman Buster Robinson. My legs were in the water. I raised my head and watched them bob about down there in the wake from ferries and tugs, in the slurry of candy wrappers, paper cups and other flotsam that had collected around them.

Stories, then.

The ones I moved through those first days on the street, as I lowered myself into the depths, heading downtown.

Just off Tchoupitoulas above Napoleon, where train tracks shrug shoulders into the river's curve, I came across a group of elderly black men sitting on the bank around a galvanized tub of iced beer and a bowl of cold fried chicken. Most had homemade fishing poles and mostly they wore polyester pants with ribbed white underwear shirts or old dress shirts with wayward collars, thin nylon socks, black shoes. Plastic milk crates and cheap folding lawn chairs provided seats. They invited me to join them.

"Have some chicken."

"Hep yourself to a beer."

A kind of gentlemen's club, I learned, they met here each day.

Sam had been a barber down by Jackson Avenue nigh on fifty years. Rarely saw a white face down there.

Ulysses had sous-chefed all his *ad*ult life at uptown restaurants where the menus were a kind of found poetry and wine bottles proliferated like brooms in *The Sorcerer's Apprentice*.

William did whatever he could find, always had and still did, janitoring, yard work, roadwork. Lot less of *all* that now, though. Too many people driving by, knocking on doors, scavenging after what subsistence they could. He understood how that was. Wasn't about to begrudge them.

Thing was, from the time he was twelve and already on his own, William'd always given top value for your dollar. Pay for ten hours' work, you were just as likely to get twelve or fifteen or twenty out of him, whatever the job demanded. He wouldn't walk away till it was done. And there were some who remembered, some who took notice.

So William—some called him Sweet William, others Big Bad Bill, and when they did, they laughed—still got work three, four days a week. And when he *didn't* work, generally he showed up here with beer for the rest, most of whom had been without work now for years.

We sat swapping stories around the beer tub, as people once gathered around campfires.

"You do remember that Reagan fellow?" James Lee said when his turn came. He'd taught for years at Xavier, history and economics; everyone called him Professor. "One of the true heroes of our cause. 'Long with Jesse Helms, of course."

America's memory is short. Abjuring any sense of history, the nation eternally improvises itself. Highwaymen such as Richard Nixon disappear only to emerge years later as "elder statesmen." A presidential candidate recently referred to Ronald Reagan as the best president this country ever had. All over America, jaws dropped. But (and this is the amazing part) just as many didn't.

"Yassuh, we be retired, the mosta us," one of the company said. Fishing a beer from the tub, he opened it. It spewed, provoking general laughter.

"What we are all right."

"*Re*tired."

"Tired and tired again."

"Like that beer. Make some rude noise, then go back to what we can't help being."

"American-dream word, ain't it, retired?"

All those big words that make us so unhappy. Stephen Daedalus was right to fear them.

"Some day these fish ain' bitin'—"

"Thass *most* days, Sheldon."

"You right, ole man."

"—we goan hafta study *collectin*' all them words. Make us up a list. Regular devil's dictionary. *E*-quality. *De*-mock-racy. Damn. Just roll right *off* the tongue, don't they?"

"They do for sure."

More than one voice: "Yeah!"

We'd cut right to call and response, echoes of talking drums in Congo Square and church amens, the slapshot syllogism at the heart of the blues.

"You want this last piece a chicken, Lewis?" Sam the barber said. "Think we all 'bout had our fill."

One last volley, then: "Life, liberty—"

"And the pursuit of happiness."

"You mean haplessness, don't you, *Eugene*?" The Professor's eyes met mine. We were both in hiding—in plain sight, like Poe's purloined letter.

By this time chickens were nibbled down to dry bone, beer had become a couple dozen empty cans floating in tepid water and fish (if indeed they'd ever entertained such a notion) had given up biting. The day itself, ebbing away in pink-and-gray dribbles on the horizon, abandoned all illusion, all pretense: knew once again it wouldn't survive. The group began dispersing. I bade them good-bye.

Then, following river's bend into what used to be called the Irish Channel, I wound up (like Jesus) among thieves.

Back doors of nondescript vans open in an abandoned school parking lot, these maverick capitalists gathered over their latest takes: trading, bartering, buying and selling, avidly redistributing wealth. From time to time kids pedaled up on bicycles with baskets full of goods and pedaled away again with baskets empty.

TVs were a major commodity, as were portable stereos, VCRs, CD players and boom boxes.

Lots of laptop computers these days, I noticed. Larger systems, proving difficult both to transport and to fence, generally stood untouched, but the little ones were fair game, negotiable. New technology, new crimes.

I thought how Newt Gingrich some years back told us flat out that all our country's problems would be solved once information became freely accessible on the Internet. Such sweetness to what he said, in a way: this blind, ever-renewable innocence at America's heart. The man simply could not imagine that other lives might be different from his own. One journalist looked over at the housing project across the street, wondering aloud how many of the residents had their computers turned on just then.

I slept that first night under a bench in a pie-slice park on Magazine, my bench and two others, a border of hedge and an anonymous statue pretty much comprising it. Directly across Magazine, used furniture stores stood shoulder to shoulder, tanklike steel desks and Formica dinette sets showing dimly through windows cataracted with grime. A bar took up the V's other leg, HALF MOON painted freehand on its blacked-out window, sign above the door reading THE PLACE. Chains were wound through the square bars of a security gate whose lock no

longer worked. Drifts of refuse and leaves at the gate's base bore witness
to long disuse.

Early morning—I'd stepped out of time's circle, gone to Hopi
Mean Time like Doo-Wop, give-and-take of light and body's promptings my only calendar or clock—I woke to the sound of a car idling
nearby and a voice above me.

Policeman squatting there, face through the bench's slats looking
all of sixteen years old. Telling me I'd best move along. Partner in the
car watching, hands wrapped around a plastic cup of Circle K coffee.

"You okay, sir?"

Sir? I guess some things do change.

I nodded.

"You heard me, right?"

I began climbing out from under the bench, stiff and sore from the
day's walking as much as from the night's cramped position.

"You need help? You walk okay?"

No. Yes.

"Better hit it, then. Store owners'll start showing up soon, don't much
like campers. Be on the phone in three minutes and we'd be right back
down here."

I stood, one hand on the back of the bench. Not too steady at all.
Legs simultaneously numb and knotted with cramps. Absurdly thinking
of Reagan in some old movie: My legs, what happened to my legs?

"Hey, you sure you're okay? When's the last time you ate? Don't
know how you guys pull it off. Here." He handed me a five. "But it's for
food, right? Nothing else."

I thanked him.

"No problem. Listen, you take care, okay?"

He got back in the car. The radio crackled. They had the air cranked
up high. He and partner sat watching as I moved away down Magazine.
The street turned one-way and empty here. No one coming uptown this
time of day. The whole city might be deserted. Lifeless husks of cars,
shells of buildings. I was the only one left alive.

31

LATER THAT MORNING as I walked by an empty lot on lower Prytania where an impromptu flea market had sprung up, cars, wooden pushcarts and shopping carts spilling out lines of tools, cardboard boxes of record albums, ground cloths or improvised tables laid with waffle irons, hot dog cookers and coconuts turned into heads with shells for eyes, I thought how much of my life these past forty-plus years, since I came to New Orleans, had been passed simply moving through the city, watching it close and reopen like some huge wood-and-stone flower around me, forever new, forever the same; and how much, on the other hand, passed as I sat afloat, apart and alone, a distracted Archimedes, in my room.

All these years I'd believed I understood the city's real life—conceit of the worst sort. Whole generations of change had passed outside, fogging the glass with their breath as they peered in, some of them knocking at the pane, as I sat writing my own books and reading others, sunk in the dailiness of my life. Pascal claimed that all man's unhappiness arises from the single fact that he is unable to remain quietly in his own chamber. Hedging the bet again.

Appropriately enough, I thought of Hamsun's *Hunger*, how on a gloomy, wet morning the novel's protagonist departs with his few yet-unpawned possessions rolled into a blanket, promising in a note left behind to his landlady that soon enough, away from these distractions and with time to scribble out a scatter of *feuilletons* for the local paper, he'll remit not only her due but a handsome interest as well.

I thought, too, of the immense sadness of Rimbaud's last letter, dictated to his sister the day before his death. I imagine her at bedside, taking this down, then, as Arthur falls back into pure delirium (I smell her soap-washed body, the stench of his decomposing leg and sour, acid sweat, unguents and incense set out to cover these), stepping to the door where Mother waits, saying, Perhaps he will rest now.

> I wish to change today from this steamship service, which I do not even know the name of, but in any case let it be the Aphinar line. All those lines are everywhere here; and I, powerless, unhappy, can find nothing; the first dog you meet in the street will be able to tell you.
>
> So send me the list of fares from Aphinar to Suez. I am completely paralysed: therefore I wish to be embarked early. Tell me at what time I must be carried on board.

Crossing Canal, prow of my own *bateau ivre* breaking through floes of tourists in fanny packs and sensible shoes consulting city maps and Greyline schedules, I moved downstream towards the river's thirsty mouth. Where paddle-wheelers kept slow count of bodies walking planks into them and ferries struck out every half hour, swimming frantically overhand, for far Algiers. Slaves fresh from Africa were held there before being brought over to the Quarter for sale. Everything they knew and understood was gone. Stacked belowdeck like logs, awash in their own refuse, they'd emerge blinking, caked with grime and reeking. So much for the joys of a sea cruise.

Amazing Floridas! Hideous wrecks at the bottom of brown gulfs! Every dawn—every last one of them—heartbreaking.

Here I am now on Decatur, walking narrow sidewalks beneath balconies off the apartments above, past bars with front doors propped open and cats aperch on rear half-doors into kitchens through which can be ordered shrimp, special luncheon plates, fried onions, peppers and potatoes, muffalettas heaped with olive salad, thick po-boys, daiquiris, beer.

Here again, walking up Esplanade in thrall to gentrification. Security gates, doormen and keypads everywhere in evidence now, where brief years ago columns on swayback porches had burst with onion plants and whole floors been chopped indiscriminately (bathtubs in kitchens, walls of sagging plywood) into low-rent rooms.

On into the Faubourg Marigny. After several decades' disuse and crumble, shotgun houses down here again are inhabited, bikes, motorcycles and hibachis out front bespeaking occupation, clothes and hammocks hung from lines and fences out back confirming it, new paint, new cement steps. No trees or greenery. Houses like books on a shelf. This part of the city resoundingly gay. Strips of alternative bookstores, vintage clothing shops, specialty restaurants, bars and galleries, a fine storefront theater, perhaps most of all the headquarters for NO Aids, make a true neighborhood of it—one in which Richard Garces felt at home. Making me wonder what neighborhood, what community, *I* might ever feel at home in.

None, maybe. God knows I'd tried enough of them.

Years ago I'd bitten off a part of the great American dream I could never swallow. I was still chewing on it.

"Tween what we see, what be," John Berryman wrote in *The Dream Songs*, "is blinds. Them blinds' on fire."

Convenience kills, I'd seen spray-painted on the side of a K&B.

And I, powerless, unhappy, could find nothing to put out the fire. Ask the first dog you meet in the street.

That second night I slept in the Faubourg's block of a park, wakened just past dawn by the rattle of chains being unwound from steel gates. Someone stood over me looking down. I heard his breath coming and going, smelled the cup of coffee he'd just drunk, traces of musk from early-morning sex. Should he speak or keep his peace?

(Why do you cry? Are we not happy? Nietzsche asks, momentarily catching the eye of the sister who cares for him.

No, Friedrich, we're not. Nor will we ever be. Children afraid of the night who have never been happy or good.)

I listened to the park guardian's footsteps pass away, noting how he kept to grass, avoiding cement walks. In one of the apartments overlooking the park a fresh cup of coffee, a baguette or pretzel put into the oven to warm, a lover or companion, awaited him.

I started back up Frenchmen towards the Quarter.

Forlorn horn from the river just blocks away. Some outbound ship awaiting bodies.

Tell me at what time I must be carried aboard.

32

T H A T   W H O L E   D A Y I strayed through the city, seeing it as though for the first time. Fresh off one of the ships, without even language to contain this experience, codify it. A painter once remarked that seeing consists of forgetting you know the name of the thing that's seen.

I remembered the voiceover beginning Tavernier's *Deathwatch* and circling back at the end. Harvey Keitel's eyes have been replaced with cameras. Everything towards which he turns his head now is captured, caught: he's become the ultimate artist. "He told me he spent that whole day walking . . ." Keitel like Oedipus by movie's end, blind yet—because from some immeasurable mix of guilt and love he chose that blindness—humanized.

Soon too, like Keitel's character, I found myself in a mission, upper bunk near the back of the dorm, after a dinner of vegetable soup heavy on cabbage and white beans, two slices of white bread piled atop, mug of coffee, the whole of it consumed in the shade of your basic Fundamentalist ranting. Recalling all those youthful Sundays back home, packed into my suit (pajamas worn under, suit scratchy wool like Mom's army-surplus blankets) and clip-on tie, pantseat polishing hardwood pews under stained-glass windows illustrating the parable of the talents, Jesus bringing in sheaves, the prodigal son, stone rolled back from the tomb.

I'd been here before. Last Thursday, following up on the list Richard Garces gave me. The guy who finally admitted *well, yes, he did kind of look after things* (nowhere in evidence now, I noticed) had shown me around, guided me to boxes of books stacked in the hall by his own cramped room.

It all looked substantially different now, of course. Perspective is everything.

Lights-out was at ten. Then you lie listening to bodies turn on the spit of their memories, volleys of farts from newly challenged digestive systems, the occasional scream or convulsion, conversations so private that only one person's involved. You feel the rasp of coarse blankets, monitor the thunderlike rumbling of your own bowels. You're asleep, then awake, then asleep again but aware you're dreaming: another border given way.

What time of night is it? No way to know. Have you slept an hour? Four hours? Ten minutes?

A single bare bulb hung at the back of the hall, eclipsed as pilgrims shuttled back and forth to the bathroom. Then they'd settle back into beds hawking, hegiras having stirred up various sediments in chest and head.

Never more alone than at 3 A.M. Wake without reason, night's face staring you down. ERs fill with patients. Men my age suddenly alert, certain that the pain in their arm's a heart attack.

Dim residual light from outside, lash of car headlights. Someone moving below me. A voice.

"You okay up there, man?"

"What?"

"Been slam-dunkin' yourself for the better part of an hour now."

"Sorry."

"Hey. No problem. God knows I'm used to it."

"Come here often, do you?"

"Regular Soup Kitchen Sam, yeah."

"Don't guess you know what time it is."

If I'd had a brother, this was the way it might have felt. Parents elsewhere in the house. Two of us up here in the crow's nest holding out against the world.

"Three-eighteen."

Okay. So that morning light in the window's only imagination. Too much night left.

"Name's Griffin, right?"

A beat went by. Two beats.

"Word is, you're a good man. What everyone says. What they don't know is why you'd be down here now, way you are."

I give up. Don't know, myself.

"My grandmother used to tell me how this collector'd come 'round. Tell her records show she owed some arrears. He'd stay to drink a cup of coffee, then after he was gone she'd lift up the napkin, find a five-dollar bill there."

"Heard the same story about Pretty Boy Floyd."

"Right. People be callin' you Pretty Boy Griffin soon." He laughed. It sounded like someone choking. "You ain't though."

"Pretty boy?"

Same laugh. Neither of us said anything for a while. Lay listening to the bodies around us.

"Grandmother raised me. Neither one of us ever knew where my mother might've got off to. Never developed much feeling for people—maybe because of that, who knows? Mostly dog meat, from my experience. Scrape out the bowl. But I purely loved that woman."

One of our shipmates lunged past, bouncing from bed to bed, and fetched up against the wall, where he began sonorously throwing up. Raw-meat smell of blood.

"Gran's life was hard. Wasn't much ever came along to ease it."

We fell asleep again.

Then, five or so, some fool decided his destiny was to liberate whatever I'd squirreled away in my bunk and came rooting. I heard him four steps off. I'd just clamped a fist around his balls when a hand snaked down from the bunk above, wrapped hair about itself and lifted. The would-be hijacker's eyes went round. Feet half a foot off the floor.

"Your call," my bunkmate said. "What'll we do with this piece a shit?"

"What the hell. Turn him loose, I guess."

"You sure?"

"Yeah."

"Not much fun in that, is there?" But he set him down.

The hijacker scuttled away.

Light had begun breaking outside. Real this time, not imagined. We lay there wide awake.

"Be routing us for breakfast soon enough," my bunkmate said. "You up for slimy grits, soggy toast and half-done eggs?"

"I've handled worse."

"Bet you have."

Roused by light and smells from the kitchen, without real purpose, direction or goal, bodies had begun staggering about, a kind of Brownian motion.

"Don't mean to impose. Your life and your business. But why *are* you down here?"

"Trying to find myself."

"Bad thing to lose."

"Have to admit it takes some doing." Or maybe not, come to think of it.

Meanwhile, things had picked up in the kitchen.

"Smell that coffee. No better smell in the world." Spoken like a true New Orleanian.

"One tip for you, though."

"Okay."

"Don't touch the casseroles or macaroni. Pasta here'll kill you. It's documented."

33

SIMPLE SUZIE WAS around fifty now, my age, a little less. She'd been on the street for twenty years at least, and everyone knew her: cops, mail carriers, newspaper boys, homeowners and apartment renters on her usual beat just riverside of Claiborne in the triangle formed by Felicity and Melpomene, enclosing Terpsichore, Euterpe, Polymnia. Some of these people gave her food, others asked about her dog Daniel. Daniel had been dead as long as she'd been on the streets, but she still talked about him all the time. For eight, ten years Suzie's husband beat her every other day or so. Then one day he came home from work early (he'd been fired but failed to tell her that) and because she didn't have dinner ready (at four in the afternoon) grabbed Daniel up by the hind legs and swung him against the wall. Dog barely had time to bark twice. And when Suzie bent over the dog, something like oatmeal with ketchup coming out its ears and broken skull, he started in on her. When neighbors checked a couple of days later she was still lying there in the kitchen. Went to Charity and hadn't been the same since. That's when she became Simple Suzie and a denizen of New Orleans' streets, as famous in her own uptown way as Sam the Preacher or the Duck Lady in the Quarter. Police never found the husband.

As he struggled up the slope towards sixty, Ed opened the door one day to an unexpected visitor: no word for it then, but now we call it Alzheimer's. Within a year things had got bad enough that he couldn't live alone anymore and moved in with his only daughter and her husband. Within two, things were bad enough that he couldn't do much of anything on his own. Dress himself, for instance, or see to personal hygiene. And within three, daughter Cassie had died, leaving husband Al (for Aloysius, but no one God help him knew that) with three kids under ten, Grandpa Ed and a job that paid three-sixty-five an hour. The kids pretty much fended for themselves as Al began coming home later and later from work. Then one day he didn't come home at all. Couple of days after, Ed realized he was hungry, no one had been bringing him food. He pried off a simple window lock. Using the lock as a lever, a closet doorknob as a hammer, he worked the pins out of the door hinges. He went downstairs into the family room, where the kids, startled at the appearance of this naked old man smeared in his own excrement (though in fact they looked much the same), began screaming. Ed walked on into the kitchen, found a box of grits and some dodgy cheese, threw it all together in a pan to cook. While it did so, he called the police. Spent a few months over at Mandeville, then was released. The hospital delivered him to a halfway house on Jackson. Smiling and yessiring the whole time, he checked in, went through the door of the room he was to share with three others, and right out the window. Now, still smiling, still yessiring the whole time, he was one of those guys you saw going through the trash you'd put out curbside. These days he had quite a wardrobe he'd retrieved from those trash cans, and showed up on the streets each morning in a new outfit.

After class one day Professor Bill bent down to pick up a book one of his graduate students had dropped and felt something pop in his chest, a spontaneous pneumothorax, as it turned out. Within moments he had difficulty breathing. Paramedics were called, he was taken to nearby Oschner, chest tubes were inserted to relieve pressure, and he wound up on a ventilator in the medical ICU. Hours later, difficult breathing made a curtain call: another pneumo, another chest tube. Further complications ensued. Four months along, chiefly at the urging of his insurance carrier, at last off the ventilator and doing well, Professor Bill was transferred to a long-term facility for rehabilitation. That very night a bullet from a drive-by shooting a block away penetrated the wall of Bill's room and his chest, all but severing his vena cava. Blood and the oxygen it carried drained away from his brain. Only the intervention of an eighteen-year-old orderly, who recognized what was happening and thrust his fingers into the leaking vessel, saved Bill from death. This all happened ten years ago. Now Bill spent his days wandering about down-town, occasionally lecturing passersby on street corners or patrons in Wendy's and Winchell's on early American military history, most often not speaking at all.

As Buster Robinson would have said: Long after midnight when death comes slipping in your room, you gonna need somebody on your bond.

Or Gnostics: If you find a way of getting out what is within you, it can save you; if you don't, it will kill you.

But often enough it won't matter how hard you listen for the universe's voice outside you, for the still, small voice of truth inside.

Often enough, no matter what you do, the wind's footsteps are all you'll hear.

34

THE CITY HAD followed Rimbaud's advice: *Je est un autre.* "I" is
another. Or maybe it was just that *I* had become another. Which I guess
was pretty much young Arthur's point. Everything had changed because
I had changed. The shape of the jar defines what is contained. We can
say only what language allows us to say. And to say more we must change
language itself. It was a quest Rimbaud finally fled, taking his sad,
doomed refuge in Abyssinia. But he'd almost done it. He'd bent language almost, *almost*, into new shapes—before it sprang back.

And now I was in a kind of Abyssinia myself.

Soon enough I'd lost all sense of time; I might just as easily have
been on the streets a week, six or eight weeks, months on end. Not that
anything was lost. On the contrary, each moment was scored deeply into
my memory. That very immediacy mitigated time's flow. Days and time
of day had become irrelevant. Only the moment mattered.

I pass from missions doling out watery soup and day-old bread
donated by Leidenheimer Bakery to others where we queue for beds
(take a number please) till available spaces are filled (shipwreck victims
awaiting allocation to lifeboats), to squatters' pads in abandoned, half-
demolished buildings reeking of fresh human refuse and decomposing
foodstuffs, to curiously medieval communities pitched beneath the
vaults of passovers and bridges and Villonesque thieves' societies met
in the cloisters of canal culverts.

I sleep upon benches and beneath them, in the recess of doorways, at the foot of hedges set out sentrylike alongside public parks, public buildings, apartment complexes, unreclaimed lots.

Days, I walk. Walk uptown on Carrollton to Oak or Freret or Maple, along St. Charles from Broadway to Napoleon to Jackson, downtown following the curve of the river to Esplanade then hopscotching back up through the Quarter, lakeward on Canal past shopfronts topped with boarded-up vacant spaces and across Basin, what used to be Storyville. Walk as though, for the city to keep its existence, not fade away, it must daily, hourly, ceaselessly be traced over, repaced, reaffirmed.

One afternoon I found myself on Prytania. Sitting on the steps of a recently renovated, still-unoccupied double across the street, through the front windows of my old house I watched Zeke step from table to mantel and back again, speaking animatedly with someone out of sight, huge ceramic mug in his hand. An early dinner, perhaps, just now finished. Or tea. A variety of containers, plates and bowls were set out. Zeke picked up a book from the table, opened it and read aloud. A hand and lower arm came into view, narrow wrist, slim fingers entwined about the stem of a wineglass. Then for the second time a police car cruised slowly by and I knew it was time to pick up my bag of belongings and move along.

Another afternoon, could have been the next, or weeks later, or a month (no seasons here in New Orleans to help orient us to passing time, not even that, only the ticking over of day and night), I found myself sitting on the levee with a man whose face I knew. We both had our heels spurred into the ground and sat crouched over, knees in the air. He had a bag of food he'd salvaged from the Dumpster out behind Frankie's in the riverbend: a mélange of fried shrimp, garlic toast, pasta and fish, soggy, forlorn fries, broccoli and carrots, even half a steak. I had a plastic bottle I'd filled with water at an Exxon station and four beers I'd filched from a car whose driver stopped off at Lenny's News-stand for a paper and left the windows down.

I tore one of the beers free of its plastic webbing and handed it to my companion. Nodding thanks, he worked the can into the dirt beside him, digging out a niche for it. On the back of a pizza carton he carefully set out for me four shrimp, portions of pasta, three pieces of fish, fries, a watery mound of broccoli and carrots and something else, mirliton maybe. Nothing to cut the steak with, so I'd have to wait till he'd had his share, then he'd pass it along.

Down on that shining blade of water a barge the size and shape of an aircraft carrier inched upriver. Behind us, at the base of the levee, car after slow car, a train clanked by. A small plane caught and threw sunlight as it coasted through clouds. Everybody, everything going somewhere, it seemed.

We ate. And when my companion held the empty can high over his mouth to drain out the last drop, I handed him another beer. He looked momentarily surprised, hesitated before accepting it.

"Obliged," he said. Among the first words to pass between us.

"You a reader by any chance?" I asked once we'd eaten awhile.

He grunted and took a sip of beer. Pulled a paperback from his back pocket. It was a perfect mold of his buttock. An ancient, off-size Avon edition that originally sold for 35 cents, *The Real Cool Killers* by Chester Himes.

I took the book and looked through it. It was well paged, sentences roughly underlined, words scribbled in margins. My companion had been doing research, as he had with *The Old Man*, creating a life for himself.

"Always loved books myself, from the very first, early as I can remember. Used to hold them up in front of me, couldn't of been more than four, five years old, pretend I was reading. What I'd done was memorize them, word for word."

"Yeah? Well, good on you. That's what Brits say. Good on you."

He drank off half the remaining beer in a gulp, made a spoon of two fingers to scoop up vegetables.

"Always liked that, good on you."

"See your point. Somehow that really says it, doesn't it?"

My companion nodded. "Good on you." His eyes peered into the middle distance, lost in memory. "Doubled up for a time with a Brit. We looked out for each other, done for each other, you know? This was some years back. Nights we'd lie there and he'd start telling me all these things he knew. Things out of books. Greek plays, the Lake Poets, Christopher Smart and what Sam Johnson said about him, old Bertie Russell. *We're* the true hollow men, the stuffed men, he'd say, headpieces filled with straw. Rat's feet over broken glass in our dry cellars and like that. Nigel, his name was. Smartest man I ever knew or'm likely to."

For a moment, again, his eyes went away.

"Thing was, Nigel truly loved his drink. One day we were sitting at a bus stop on Magazine, just getting out of the heat for a minute, you know, not half a mile from where we are right now, when a cab pulls over and a man in a pinstripe suit gets out to go into an antique store. Nigel says, the way he always would, Good day t'you, and this stops the guy dead in his tracks, cause he's British too, you see. They talk awhile and the man pulls out his wallet and hands Nigel a fifty-dollar bill. Nigel, he just sits there staring at it. Good on you, Nigel says to him finally. Good luck to you, ta, the man says.

"We went straight over to the K&B on St. Charles, Nigel and I did, and we bought a gallon of cheap gin, another of bourbon, three or four six-packs of Ballantine beer. Had them put it in proper bags and everything. Nigel stood there folding and unfolding that bill and folding it up again. Counted his change half a dozen times at least, once he'd turned it over.

"I don't remember a lot else. Not much of a drinking man back in those days, and all that alcohol hit me hard. I came 'round sometime that evening. Fireflies, what we always called lightning bugs when I was a kid, blinked here and there. 'Searching for an honest man,' I remember Nigel said. 'Like Diogenes.' His voice sounded funny. 'Rest of this money's yours now, I guess.' Eight dollars and some jingly. 'You been a good mate, Robert Lee.' I don't recall anyone else ever calling me by name, not for years.

"I walked over there by him and he was laying 'cross the tracks. And the whole bottom of him, waist on down, it was like one a them ventriloquist dummies, nothing much left there, just this flat, floppy stuff. He'd passed out on the tracks and a train had run over him.

"They did what they could at Touro—that was the closest hospital, where they took him. But he passed on later that night. I was sitting watching a old movie on TV, something with Jimmy Stewart, when the doctor came out and told me. For a long time all I could think of was Nigel saying to me, You been a good mate, Robert Lee. Last best friend I had. Last friend period."

"Look," I said after a decent amount of time had passed, "I don't mean to get too personal here, don't want to crowd you, but I know you."

"Don't see how. 'Less you caught me on Johnny Carson last week, that is."

Carson, of course, hadn't been on in years.

"From the picture on your books. *The Old Man, Mole, Skull Meat*. I've worn out four or five copies of every one of them, gave away as many more to friends. You're Lew Griffin."

He scooped up another mouthful of vegetables. "You think so?" Washed them down with a hit of beer. "Griffin, you say. Griffin." He shook his head. "I don't know. Maybe I used to be. My old man used to say here in America we could be anything we wanna be. Yeah, right. But I don't remember much these days. What I do remember, it comes in spurts, same as my pee does. Stand there five, ten minutes before it lets go. Then everything shuts down again. Can't even much say as I want to remember, not really."

He ran fingers across a permanent stubble of beard. Dry skin flaked off onto his shirt.

"Griffin . . ."

His eyes strayed again, grappled after footholds somewhere among things of the world, river, meal, clouds, sun.

" 'In the darkness things always go away from you. Memory holds you down while regret and sorrow kick hell out of you,' " I prompted.

"Well, *that*'s the truth for sure." He scooped up what remained of the vegetables, a greenish paste nearly as appetizing as baby food from the jar. "Don't guess you'd have any more a these beers?"

He well knew I did. I tore the next-to-last one free of its webbing.

"Obliged."

We sat quietly together. Plane, boat and train gone now. Sky, river, tracks and street all empty. Closest thing to silence you'll find in a city.

"Guess, some point or another, you musta had hell kicked out of you too, be my guess," he said.

"You'd be right."

"Sure I would. Good beer." He held up the can. "Don't mean to be hoggin' it, mind." He handed the can to me. I drank and returned it. He set it down again in the niche he'd made for it. "You from around here?"

"Coming onto thirty-five years. Not much more than a kid when I moved here. Guess it's home by now."

"Guess it is. Never spent much time anywhere else myself, mind. Love this goddamn city. Ain't always been easy, though. Ever' few years, city gets to be a real motherfucker. Mess your mind up good. Break your heart."

"Yeah."

We sat quietly side by side. The sun was beginning to set. New Orleans doesn't go in much for twilight. Sun there on the horizon one moment, light still good, ten minutes later it's nighttime.

"We've met before," I said. "You don't remember."

He shook his head.

"Hotel Dieu. You'd been beaten pretty severely. Everyone thought a truck had run over you. I don't know when this was—a while back— but you were pretty bad off. They weren't sure you were going to make it for a while there. Then you left. Just got up one day and walked out."

"Can't say as I remember any of that. Sorry."

"Sorry?"

"Sounds like it might be important to you. Sorry I can't help." He held out the beer can. "You want the last of this? Dance with the one you brought?"

No.

"You had a book with you. At the hospital." I rummaged in my bag and pulled it out. "This one."

He took it from me, looked at the cover, then turned it over to read the back cover. Held it like a deck of cards, fanning his thumb along the edge back to front, riffling pages. Several pages all but separated themselves.

"Later, when you asked, I left my notebook with you."

I exchanged book for notebook. He browsed through, turning pages at random.

"That's your writing. All but the first four or five pages."

"Yeah. Could be, I guess. Not so's I can remember, mind you. Definitely strange. Places I recognize in here, people I know I've come across, sure. Not much to tie it all together though, is there?"

"Not a lot. But you do remember the book, the notebook, writing in it . . ."

"Maybe. Hard to say."

He held the beer can against his ear as one might a seashell.

"Not much I can depend on these days. Too much of it gets away from me. Just slips away and I never even know it was there." He held up the empty can, looking at it. What *does* one do with a thing like this? "Hotel Dieu."

"Supposed to be called University Hospital now, but no one does."

"Something back there in the shadows for sure. Be a hell of a time pulling it out, though. Nudge it into daylight, stand up straight, tell us about yourself. You were there, you say."

I nodded.

"I remember I was pushing my boat up the Nile. All these little sucking kisses on my skin where leeches were attaching themselves. I was living off some hard, bitter-tasting fruit off trees on the bank and the raw flesh of fish with teeth like razors that I snared in nets improvised from old shirts. Had these big grins on them."

His own drunkboat, his own *African Queen*.

"All these people were after me. They wouldn't give up. Never even knew who they were. See them, feel them, back there behind me. Someone pulled a tube out of my throat."

"You were on a ventilator for a while. A breathing machine. I was there when they took you off."

"All at once I had to breathe again. Had to go on. Before, it had been so easy."

"Always that choice."

"We spoke, didn't we? Something about a missing son, old man looking for him. Ever find him?"

I shook my head. "No."

Night had not so much fallen about us as it had toppled there, collapsed, capsized. Lights lashed up from boats on the river, others stabbed at the darkness from cars racing past on Leake Avenue behind us.

"Someone else brought news—or no news. They drank together."

"Right. The detective and the old man, the father who'd hired him. In a bar on Decatur. Detective's come to tell him his son is dead."

" 'Nothing to help us but a few hard drinks and morning.' I *do* remember that. You the one read it to me?"

I shook my head again.

"Someone else, then. I was terrible sick, some kind of flu, burning up one minute, freezing the next. Let go in the bed a couple of times I know of at least, too weak to crawl out. Guess he probably cleaned that up too, in between reading this book to me, spooning soup down me. Had to be a week at least, I was like that. He must of read that book to me cover to cover half a dozen times."

"Don't suppose you remember what he looked like."

"Not paying much attention at the time. Not quite there, right?

Couldn't get outside myself. Young man's what I see now I look back on it."

"Black or white?"

"Black. Like you. Mostly his eyes I remember."

"His eyes."

"Brown. With green floating around somewhere in there, never could say just how or where. Like yours."

"Ever hear his name?"

He thought it over. "Sorry. Can't recall his ever using one. Not much use for names, situations like that."

"He never introduced himself? Hi, I'm Carl, I'll be your waiter for today?"

"He could have. Like I say, I was pretty far gone."

"Never heard another staff member speak to him, maybe call him by name?"

He shook his head. "I think I'd remember. Whole thing's etched in my mind. Like a dream, doesn't make much sense, but you can't shake it off, can't get shed of it. I thought I was dying. Held on pretty hard to whatever I could grab on to. Strange times."

Dark now was absolute.

"One more beer, you want it," I said.

"You don't?"

"Got your name on it."

"Why not, then."

First he rolled it along his forehead, then popped it open and drank.

"One thing," he said.

"Yes?"

"Never thought of this before."

I waited.

"When I first started coming out of it. Most of it's kind of a blur, you understand, what happened when, the order of things. All jumbled up together. But now I think about it, there was this one time I came half awake—early morning, late evening, no way to tell—and someone's standing there over me saying, You're going to be okay, you hear me, you're going to be okay, it's just a matter of time now.

"I remember reaching up, things still not too clear. Didn't know him. Could be one of those who'd been chasing after me. My hand's huge up there, blots out the whole sky. I try to ask him. He takes my hand and bends close over me.

Now his face fills the sky. Can't make out what I'm saying.

" 'David?' he says, 'You're asking after David? He's gone on. Sicker ones than you here now, mate. But not to worry: we'll take good care of you.' "

35

WELCOME BACK.

Yeah, I guess you *could* say the same to me. But neither of us's ever really been away, have we?

Abyssinia, right. Turns out it looks just like Metairie, except with camels. We drag our worlds along with us and we can't let them go, can't get rid of the damned things. Trapped animals have better sense. They'll gnaw a leg off and crawl away. We just tell ourselves that once we get the furniture inside our heads rearranged it's going to be a new room, a new world. Sure it is.

But you're going to be okay, Lewis. We both are.

You've been here just over three weeks. Don't suppose you remember much of it. Police picked you up finally. You'd been sitting on curbs outside Cooter Brown's and a string of bars up on Oak berating customers as they came out, demanding what you kept calling donations, going in these places and, before they heaved you back out, grabbing half-finished beers and drinks off the tables.

Sound familiar?

You still feel like you're underwater looking out, what you told me a few days ago, it's because the doctors have you on some pretty heavy sedation. You've been off IVs a couple of days now. You were so dehydrated when you got here you could barely pull your tongue away from the roof of your mouth. Another day or two now, you might even be able to keep food down again. Be a while before you're up for boudin or grillades, I'm afraid.

Much of those last weeks come back to you?

Well, maybe some of it will, in time. You never know. What does it matter? You're here, you survived. That's the important thing.

Okay. You're right, it *does* matter. And not only to you.

You sure you want to hear this again now? I've already told you twice.

Three, four in the morning, I had a phone call. Dan the Man two flights down, I hear him stomping up stairs like he's driving railroad spikes with his feet, everyone in the house awake for sure and lying there listening to this, no way anyone's gonna sleep through it. Then there's this polite knock at the door: You got a call Brother.

Brother's what most people call me here. Started out like so many things do as a joke, someone going Hey, bro, because I was black, someone else picking it up, calling me Brother Theresa.

I'd never had a call before.

Guy on the other end tells me his name is Richard Garces.

No, I didn't know him, only met him last week. But he told me how over the years he'd built up this loose network of people like himself, social workers, mental-health nurses and techs, people he'd talk to over the net on a regular basis, and how some years back he'd started hearing things he got curious about. So he pushed a little, asked a few strategic questions and kept his ears open, started putting it together.

Hardest thing he ever did, he said, not telling you. But he had to figure it was my own life—that I had my reasons which Reason could not know, and so on.

But that night on the phone he told me things had gone upside down. "Lew might have said *bouleversé*." And that he thought I should know.

Ten minutes tops, I was on my way. They were holding you at University Hospital pending court hearing. Don Walsh came in not long after. Didn't say much. Just shook hands, a little sadly I thought (I didn't learn about Danny till later), and introduced his friend from the DA's office, woman named Arlene. Arlene's wearing jeans and a pink dress shirt with a man's tie at half-mast and a leather fanny pack. Steps through, around and past legal formalities like she's off somewhere else reading a book or having a good meal this is so simple, and before any of us know it we're out the other side. Standing on the sidewalk with this miserable six-in-the-morning rain slopping down us and into clogged gutters. Whole city starting to smell like wet sheep.

You and Deborah been together long?

Just wondered. She was there too by then. Asked if it were possible the two of you might be alone awhile. She had her car, she'd bring you round to the Center.

Three weeks, or just over. You came in on a Sunday. It's Monday now. Late afternoon.

Funny. I never imagined I might be sending out smoke signals, to Richard Garces or anyone else. Makes me remember what you wrote: "Signals we're set here to read."

I *did* keep track of your books. Every new one that came out I'd read it, thinking: Okay, he's managed to pull it off one more time. I'd try to figure out the people I knew, which of your apartments you were describing, the bars and restaurants and women you wrote about. *The Old Man*'s still my favorite.

You all right? Need to rest? That's some strong stuff you're behind right now. Know how it is.

Maybe later we'll have the chance, be able, to talk about all that.

Remember how when I was a kid you used to recite the prologue to *The Canterbury Tales* to me in Middle English, tell me about Rimbaud? *Je est un autre.* You must become a seer. *Il faut que vous changer votre vie.*

Okay, *changiez*. Present subjunctive. Whatever. Hey: I was close.

I used to think a lot about that story you were always telling. How back home your father took you to breakfast one morning at Nick's, on the levee by the river, and how once you'd ordered and got your plates through a side window into the kitchen and were sitting there on the steps of the old railway station, watching all the white folks so warm at the tables inside and balancing greasy paper plates on knees shaky with cold he told you that no matter what you did—raise his children for him, fight his wars for him, keep his economy afloat—to the white man you'd always be invisible.

Mirrors weren't made for the likes of us, you said.

But of course I knew there was no way *I* was going to be kept away from those mirrors. Mirrors, hell. I'd be on the covers of their goddamned magazines.

We're kids, stuff like that goes through us like water. What's my old man know? Or your old man? *Any* old man. Things are different now. World's different. *I'm* different. Sure.

So I go on reading my books and then one day, it seems all at once now when I look back on it, how the hell did this ever happen, there I am, in Europe, halfway to being an old man myself.

Biggest damn mirrors you ever saw. Here's everything I've been taught is most important, everything I've made so much a part of my own life, of what I am. European art, European history, European literature, everything that defines the culture I live in. Put out a hand and you touch it. Knock over some monument of unaging intellect if you're not careful.

Then one day I realize I can't see myself in those mirrors anymore. I'm simply not there. Not there at all, however hard I stare.

Because my skin is black? Because I'm not European? You tell me. *I* haven't figured it out. But everything I'd based my life on was suddenly gone.

I came back to the States only to find that this had all become every bit as alien to me now as Paris, Berlin or London, Brittany with its cattle, Kent with its sheep.

The whole country was forts now. Fort Lakeside, Fort Prytania, the Walled City of Metairie. Malls and parking lots and fast-food chains. Everybody zipping past at forty, fifty miles an hour like trapped flies banging against windows. Everybody shut away in his own little world.

And the more you're alone, the more natural seems the importance, the supremacy, of self. Other lives become little more than contrails dissolving on the sky.

Somehow, I knew, I had to break out of that tyranny. Get the windows open, learn to move slowly again, break the mirrors, embrace others' lives.

I called you twice, but couldn't figure out what to say. I waited till the machine cut off, then hung up myself. But you know that, of course. You wrote about it.

I've been here at the Center almost the whole time. Here and other places like it. Found out pretty quickly that the pain I carried around with me, thought I couldn't bear—compared with others', that pain was nothing.

These faces, they're the mirrors I can see myself in.

Every one of them.

36

"YOURS MORE THAN most, though," my son had said there in the He'p-Se'f Center out in Gentilly, on Elysian Fields, New Orleans' own Champs-Elysees, for which (like so many other things in the city) there had been all manner of grandiose plans, none of them ever within sniffing distance of fruition, the street, built at great expense, all its life little more than an interminable bus stop lined with rathole cafés and cut-rate stores, step-up cottages with cheap cement steps and gaps between thin shingles of siding hurriedly hammered on, nothing at all by way of internal walls.

Within the week I was transferred to a halfway house in midtown, a once-grand home now given to dangerously sagging porches and balconies with railings like decayed teeth, across the street from a service station recently converted to a falafel house, sheets of plywood still stacked along the side. Holding on for dear life, and for lack of any other entertainment, inmates sat out on the balconies to watch citizens come and go.

A couple of weeks later I was home, where this time Zeke, in turn, met *me* at the door.

"This is my son, Brother David," I said, and everyone laughed: Richard Garces, Don, Deborah, Norm and Ray "RM" Marcus from up the street. All of them had come to see me home. And they'd all brought food.

For the next hour or two we worked our way through, around and over pots of red beans and rice with grilled sausage, steaming gumbo from which protruded various claws and halves of bivalve shells, tasso on a bed of mixed greens, boiled crawfish. We'd covered the kitchen table with newspapers. Garces and Norm Marcus were in competition to see who could collect the biggest heap of crawfish bodies.

I'd taken one look at my own pile of bodies, all the mail that accumulated while I was away (life goes on), and dumped it in one of the boxes people had brought food in. Over the next few weeks that box would move otherwise untouched from kitchen floor to pantry to a closet shelf to the trash can I set out curbside each Tuesday and Friday.

Zeke made untold pots of coffee and, for Deborah, cup after cup of tea, which he delivered to her on a small tray complete with cream pitcher, lemon slices, vat of sugar and a demitasse spoon he'd found somewhere. Hard to tell whether she or he got the bigger kick out of it.

Music was catch as catch can. Whoever first noticed the last record, tape or CD was done went over and put on whatever he or she wanted to. I remember hearing Fats Waller, Mozart's horn and clarinet quintets, Arrested Development, Frank Sinatra punching out lounge-lizard standards (no idea how that ever got in there: not mine), Blind Willie McTell and wife, the Charlie Christian Minton sessions, Irish music recorded live at Matt Malloy's, Springsteen's *The Ghost of Tom Joad*. At one point someone even pulled out Buster Robinson's old BlueStrain record and put that on.

Hours later Don and I found ourselves sitting on the bench under the tree in the backyard, by the slave quarters. People still moved around inside the house, in the light. Dark out here. Moonlight pushing through clouds, through humidity that shelled the moon in nacreous layers, made it a pearl. A few more neighbors had shown up, a teacher or two, Sally Mara with her latest young man, the two of them all in black. Keith LeRoy wearing perfect English.

"I hope you know how happy I am for you, Lew," Walsh said. "I mean that."

"I know you do."

"So what's up? David planning to stay here awhile?"

"I hope so. I've asked him."

"Good. That's good."

Inside, Garces, Norm and RM were trading dance moves. They were about equally bad, and loving it. Heads thrown back. Laughing.

"And Deborah? How do things stand there?"

I shrugged. "We'll see. Give time time, as the twelve-steppers say."

"Yeah. Has to be tough for her, all this coming down on her at once."

"Yeah."

"No question how much she cares, you know. All she can do just to take her eyes off you in there."

Zeke pressed his face against the glass and peered out at us. Don and I waved.

"Do me a favor, don't fuck this one up, Lew."

"I'll try."

"Sure. Sure you will." After a moment he added, "I'm pulling for you."

"You always have."

"Just don't expect as much out of her, out of the rest of us, as you do from yourself."

"You're saying this to a man who three weeks ago was drinking dregs out of beer bottles, cigarette butts and all."

"Yeah, but I didn't say anything about what you *do*. I was talking about what you *expect* of yourself."

We sat together awhile without saying more. Faintly I could hear people's laughter from a neighboring yard. Some guest I didn't know stepped just outside the kitchen door to smoke, nodding politely towards Don and me. A squirrel leapt from roof's edge to banana plant, came within half an inch of not making it.

"He was a fuckup, Lew. Always had been. Lazy as overcooked spaghetti. Weak. No skills, social or otherwise. Never gave me reason to think he'd ever be anything else."

Minutes went by.

"I loved him, Lew. No one else can understand that the way you do. I miss him. Always will."

I slid my arm up over my friend's shoulder there in the close New Orleans night, in that struggle of moonlight.

37

THE STRUGGLES CONTINUE. For all of us, I guess.

Very strange to have this house full of life again.

I'm sitting here in the slave quarters looking across to the house, thinking about past months.

David stayed over a week, then another, and before long without ever discussing it we all knew he lived here. Goes off to work in the morning and comes home every night just like a businessman, taking care of the city's wounded and walking dead. Some days I go along with him.

Zeke never quite got around to moving out either. He works for the *Times-Picayune* as an investigative reporter. "Same thing I always did," he likes to tell people, "only now they let me walk around a lot more."

Walsh even moved in for a while there, most of a month, when nights got too hard, shadows too deep and thoughts of Danny crowded close. Eventually he pulled things back into place and went home. But while he was here, evenings after dinner we'd sit outside talking. Remembering back to when we first met, recalling our search for the sniper, how Don had pulled me out of the first of many hells I'd made for myself, the late-night call when I learned that Don's wife had left him and taken the kids, David's disappearance, Danny. Beneath it all, tacitly, the way men our age do, I'm sure we were asking ourselves how all those years had got by us.

David, Zeke, Walsh. A couple of others too—but I'll save that.

Meanwhile, something extraordinary sits on the desk beside me. I've spent almost six weeks, night and day, working on this, and now I have no idea what I'll do with it.

Look back at page 1 and you'll see how I tried to turn a letter to Vicky into a rewrite of *The Old Man*. Page 64, you'll come across me trying to transform my first meeting with LaVerne from memory to meaningful, fact to fiction. Skip on to page 69 or so and you can watch me tinker with a dream I'd had, fumbling to graft it onto Deborah's sudden appearance in my life.

Look through the published books and you'll find much the same.

What I did here, in this extraordinary thing sitting beside me, is this: I quit trying. Quit trying to finesse the failures and forfeitures of my life into fiction. To tuck people I'd loved safely away in the corners of novels. Quit trying to force patterns, however comforting and fetching and artistic these patterns might be, onto the catch-as-catch-can of what I actually lived, the rigorous disorder of my days.

This extraordinary thing is my autobiography.

And I've no idea what to do with it, no idea at all.

Publishers aren't likely to be interested in an account so plain and unembellished, so *down*, so apart. Should I publish it as fiction? No doubt my editors (though *I*'d feel it a deep dishonesty) would welcome this.

Maybe best that I simply file it away with all the other papers, all those fat files neither I nor anyone else will ever read again, its frail purpose served.

Six-forty. Almost dark. Zeke walks into the kitchen to start dinner, snaps the lights on and waves through the window above the sink.

Minutes later David shows up, home early ("misery down thirty percent in New Orleans today"), and knocks at the door with camomile tea. Dinner in an hour, he says—"Zeketime, of course," which means closer to two.

I sip the tea. Supposed to stay off caffeine. Supposed to stay off damn near everything. As though I'd had enough of it. I haven't. Haven't had enough of *any*thing yet, however long and hard the siege has been. Some nights I sit on the bench outside and I'm rendered mute, absolutely mute, by the touch of the wind on my face, by lights inside the house, how beautiful the world can be.

I loved you, Vicky, and you, LaVerne, and yes, you, Clare. Loved you all and still do. All so much a part of me now.

Like Deborah.

Home from the flower shop she stands just past the window, tall and willowy and swaying slightly (or so I will always imagine her), calling, Does Lew want to come out and play.

She showed up at the door one morning days after I came back from Nighttown.

"If it's okay with you, I thought I'd just drop my things off here and go on to work."

She handed a suitcase through the door.

"I'm running late, though—what else is new? See you tonight, Lew."

"You sure about this?"

She looked at me for a moment and nodded, then turned and broke for her car. We never spoke about it again. It's her home now as much as it's mine, David's or Zeke's.

There's another as well.

I was in the slave quarters working on this extraordinary thing, this book or whatever it turns out to be, almost done with it in fact, when David came to the door. One of those drawling New Orleans afternoons that looks to go on forever. I had door and windows propped open, a glass of iced tea close by. Flies were doing head-ons all around.

"Someone to see you, Dad."

I waved my hand, a little impatiently, I'm sure, to indicate that I was working and didn't care to be bothered.

"I know. You'll want to see her. I wouldn't interrupt you otherwise. She's in the front room."

I read the last couple of paragraphs, hit Save. Got up and went in through the kitchen. Bat appeared from nowhere, buzzed first my feet, then his nearly full bowl, urgently remonstrating. When I stepped into the front room, just past the sill, her face turned to me, and for a moment irrational fear flooded me.

It could have been, for that moment I almost believed it was, her mother watching me.

Then tears welled behind my eyes.

"Hi, Lewis," she said. "Looking pretty good for an old fart."

She stepped towards me on the bare wood floor, one step, then another. Had her mother's easy grace.

"Probably I should have called. But these days I've got in the habit of doing things on a little more personal level. If you want me to leave, I will."

I shook my head.

"I've been straight a year now. That's what I promised myself: once I made it a year, I'd see you again. I've never forgotten what you did for me, Lewis. I could use a friend. Difference is, now I can *be* a friend, too. You say the word, though, I'm out of here. I'd understand."

Mute with the beauty of the world again, with its simple pleasures, I took those three necessary steps and took Alouette in my arms.

Neither of us spoke for a while.

"When I was in the hospital, on the breathing machine, you sat beside me, for hours it seemed, and you told me about when you first met my mom, how much you loved her, and how you'd never been able to tell her that.

"Once I was off crack, then, later, off alcohol, whenever things started getting bad, I'd remember your sitting there by me, telling me all that. That's what kept me going. I just hoped someone, someday, might love *me* like that, that I'd be worth it. I saw the way your pain, your sorrow, your sense of regret got all mixed up with the love you had for her, with your tenderness, all those complicated memories, and I'd think: That's what I've cut myself off from. More than anything else I just wanted to *feel* again, Lewis."

"Whatever the cost?" I asked.

"Yes."

"Welcome back," I said to Alouette. "Welcome home."